THE TERRIBLE TWOS

ISHMAEL REED

Dalkey Archive Press

Library of Congress Cataloging-in-Publication Data:

Reed, Ishmael, 1938-
    The terrible twos / Ishmael Reed. — 1st Dalkey Archive ed.
    p. cm.
    ISBN 1-56478-226-3 (pbk. : alk. paper)
    1. United States—Politics and government—Fiction. I. Title.
    PS3568.E365T4 1999
    813'.54—dc21
                        99-35665
                        CIP

This publication is partially supported by grants from the Lannan Foundation, the
Illinois Arts Council, a state agency, and the National Endowment for the Arts, a
federal agency.

Dalkey Archive Press
Illinois State University
Campus Box 4241
Normal, IL 61790-4241

visit our website at: www.dalkeyarchive.com

Printed on permanent/durable acid-free paper and bound in the United States of America.

DEDICATION

For Bill Cook, James Earl Jones, Jerry Lieber, George Clinton, Brian Whitley, and the late Charles Davis, without whose patronage this book would not have been possible.

THE
TERRIBLE
TWOS

WASHINGTON (UPI)—Confirming what many people already felt in their bones, the Commerce Department reported Sunday the rain-poor winter of 1980–1981 produced a slew of records and near records for the nation and nearly half the states.

A Past
Christmas

1

By Christmas, 1980, the earth had had enough and was beginning to send out hints. Volcanoes roared. Fish drank nitrates and sulphur. A pandemic of sleepiness and drowsiness was sweeping the earth and scientists didn't know what to make of it. Some said that it was the coldest Christmas in memory as − 40-degree temperatures blew down from the Arctic. Greece was struck with the worst snow blizzard in thirty years, the *Times* reported. "Wolves entered towns and villages to attack livestock." Declared Prime Minister Constantine, "Greece is not equipped to meet this sort of weather." In Italy, people were fleeing Naples. The Northern Hemisphere wasn't as much fun as it used to be.

The fortieth President wears $3,000 worth of clothes including an $800 overcoat from I. Magnin. He is warm and well-fed. His friends come from Bel Air, California, where the average house sells for $800,000 and people pay $600 for a shirt and $350 for a tie and an alligator handbag goes for $1,500. His friends are warm and surfeited. During his inaugural, 50,000 hot-air balloons are set afloat. Stomach-warming Kentucky bourbon and tails are back in the White House, a *Time* magazine columnist rejoices.

Eastern circles, however, are cautious. Beer money, car dealership money, supermarket money, and drugstore money surround the President. Eastern money has never heard of this money. This money from Sacramento and Orange County where the real men wear $450 Lucchese boots. Money is as tight as Scrooge. Retailers talk of a credit squeeze, and during this season of blizzards, this cold, nasty season, the newspapers devote much advertising to quartz heaters. Millions in the United States are without heat and fires that devastate entire families occur in the wintry cities of the northeast. The President is satiated and sanguine. He dines with Brooke Astor. He is warm, eating, well-fed, smiling-smiling, well-scarfed, bundled-up and waving.

Ebenezer Scrooge towers above the Washington skyline, rubbing his hands and greedily peering over his spectacles. He shows up at the inaugural in charcoal-gray stroller, dove-gray vest, gray-striped trousers, pleated-front shirt, and four-in-hand tie. Hail First Actor, and Ms. Actorperson on your thronelike blue winged chairs, and your opulent Republican dinners, and your tailors, and your fashion designers flown in from Paris and Beverly Hills and New York, and your full-page color coverage in *Women's Wear Daily*.

How did the *Buffalo Evening News* put it? "The Wild West is Back in the Saddle Again." In the west, he campaigned as a cowboy; in the south, the crowd wept and rebel-yelled at the sight of First Actor in a Confederate uniform. Miss Nancy's beautiful white people, in the Red Room, darkies in tails passing out sour mash left and right. Thank you, Miss Nancy, said Charlie Pride.

But Wall Street is skeptical, even when the President shows up in pinstripes. The *Wall Street Journal* mischievously prints the President-elect's nightclub bills incurred between his marriages; $750 per month at the Mocambo Club and Ciro's. They remind the new President that regardless of his endorsement by the electronic evangelists, he is "a man who has seen something of life."

The President-elect says he wants Santa to leave him a tractor but isn't sure Santa can get it down the chimney. He leaves out milk and cookies for Santa anyway. His cabinet officers wear expensive watches and suits. They are comfortable, well-off even. Regardless of how high inflation remains, the wealthy will have any kind of Christmas they desire, a spokesman for Neiman-Marcus announces. Their gifts range from $100 gold toothpicks to $30,000 Rolls Royces.

Ms. Charlotte Ford is cozy. She is eating well. The family can't make it to ski country this year and so they will settle for a Christmas dinner in their New York townhouse. Lunch will be served at 2:00 P.M. There will be twelve guests, six at two tables. They will eat off of china plates. They will dine on chestnut soup and turkey. For dessert, they will enjoy chocolate souffle and mince pie. The atmosphere will be "warm and congenial." There will be two kinds of wine, red and white.

By New Year's Day, seven point eight million people will be unemployed and will do without poinsettias tied with 1940 pink lace or chestnut soup. They will be unable to attend the ski lessons this year, but they will be fighting the snow, nevertheless. On Thanksgiving Day, five thousand people line up for turkey and blackeye peas in San Francisco. In D.C., four men freeze to death during inaugural week, one on the steps of a church. The church's door is locked. It is the coldest Christmas in memory and doesn't end until Inaugural Day.

Santa Claus is ubiquitous this year. Dolly Parton appears on the cover of *Rolling Stone* in a Santa Claus outfit; a little doll Santa Claus peeks from between her bosom lines. On the cover of *Fantasy* magazine, Santa Claus appears as a robot. United Press International reports on December 23, 1980, that the Sussex County Superior Court judge gave Leroy Scholtz permission to change his name to Santa C. Claus. "About fifty children and several adults, who had crammed the courtroom to lend support to 'Santa,' broke into applause as the decision was announced, and several ran up and hugged the tall, potbellied man." But all wasn't jolly for Santa Claus during 1980 Xmas. Associated Press reported on December 19, 1980, that the 125 members of the Truth Tabernacle Church, in Burlington, North Carolina, had decided that Christmas is the work of the devil and Santa is an imposter. They said that Christmas is the birthdate of the pagan god, Tammuz, and that they would allow no Christmas trees or presents. "Santa was accused of child abuse by urging parents to buy liquor instead of clothing, of lying and saying he is Saint Nicholas, of causing churches to practice Baal religion unknowingly, and causing ministers to lie about Christ's birthday. After the charges were read and the sentence pronounced, an eight-foot dummy in a Santa suit was taken to the nearest tree and hanged as about a dozen children looked on, giggling."

On the corner of Union and Buchanan Streets in San Francisco, Santa is seen driving his reindeer and sleigh. The reindeer and sleigh are made of 6,000 pounds of ice and carved by Andrew Young.

Percy Ross, "the original Jewish" Santa Claus who gave away money to black schoolchildren on a New York Street, said, "I do it because I'm luckier than most and because every day is Christmas to me." Commented one child, "the dude's all right," Associated Press reports. United Press International says that three billion Christmas cards will be exchanged with gross sales higher than last year's 1.2 billion dollars. On the cards, Santa is depicted as a golfer, a tennis player, a long-distance runner, and a jogger. Nicholas changes with the times, running neck and neck with Jesus Christ; the Vatican would like to ruin this Saint. The writer says that Clement Clark Moore, author of "A Visit from St. Nicholas," wouldn't recognize him anymore.

In 1979 one "streetwise" Santa said, "These kids today, I'll tell you, they're seven going on forty. They're not kids for very long. When I first started as a Santa they'd believe in Santa Claus until they were about eight or nine."

The *Times* reported that Steven Jones, an assistant professor of comparative studies at Ohio State University, pro-

claimed Santa Claus a sexist fertility symbol. "There is an aura
of expectancy surrounding Santa's arrival, and he is rotund in
the same way as a pregnant woman." Jones said Santa gives
things and comes down the chimney, a characteristic of the
stork of another myth. "Santa is a male character who has
usurped a female's role."

A Christmas poll is taken of American women, 75 percent
of whom say they are sexually dissatisfied. Two ominous
headlines apear: *Arctic Air Keeps Nation Frigid*, and *After
Divorce, Who Gets Custody of Christmas?*

"An ultimate machine—a device that would mine the
moon, a planet or an asteroid and use the raw materials to
make anything anyone knows how to make including an exact
replica of itself" was described by *Science Digest* as a "Santa
Claus machine."

While combating squatters in Amsterdam, the police
bring in Santa Claus to add some humor. In England, Father
Christmas is arrested for taking photos of children and selling
them for $4.95. He is told that he can't return to his favorite
spot until after Christmas, on January 5th.

Although Dick Powell starred in a 1940s movie called
Christmas in July, the traditional beginning of the American
Christmas falls on Thanksgiving Day. Of the first Thanksgiving, Professor James Deetz has written that for three days in
1621, the Anglo settlers got up in jackboots, felt hats, and
plumes to dine on, not turkey, but *eel*, an Indian named
Squanto taught them to hunt in the creeks and swamps near
their settlements. Some local Indians contributed deer and
helped the settlers put away pumpkin soup and gallons of
booze. The first Anglo settlers had robust Elizabethan ap-
petites, liked fancy clothes, and did a considerable amount of
"wenching."

In the United States, millions of TV eyes are focused
upon the Thanksgiving Day Parade which is sponsored an-
nually by Macy's department store. Two bosses of important

retail chains watch the parade from a tinted-window, chauf-feur-driven Cadillac. Brothers Herman and George Schneider both wear top hats, black-and-white striped pants, tails, shiny black shoes. Herman rests his hands on a cane.

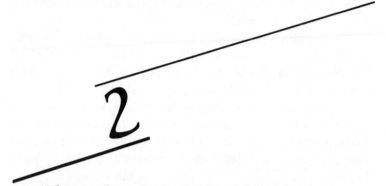

2

"This parade ought to perk up the trade," said the first boss, sipping a scotch and holding a cigar with a free hand. "Weather's just right. Maybe the industry will top the six billion we made last year."

"We'll be lucky if we break even. Things look pretty bad to me. You heard about Korvettes, didn't you? Out of business, interest rates too high. J.C. Penney's phasing out some of its stores, too. It's going to cost them fifteen million dollars to close them down," the second boss said. "It's all Carter's fault. Him and the Federal Reserve."

"Don't blame it on Carter. Blame it on the Arabs."

"The Arabs don't have long. They'll run out of oil in the late eighties and then we'll have to bail them out. You see them in Paris, dancing with French girls and in London spending cash on every frivolous thing. I heard that one of them wanted to buy the Alamo, in San Antonio, Texas."

"The Alamo? Why would he want to buy the Alamo?" A huge replica of Kermit the Frog floated by.

"Because his son went to school near there, and was

impressed with the legend of the Alamo." A group of clowns holding balloons walked by.

"We're taking a beating on those quilt down coats. The women say they can't move comfortably into their station wagons wearing those coats."

"Yeah, but the toys are selling well. Especially the computer games. There's also a rush on microwave ovens."

"If American labor made better stuff we could sell it. If it isn't sick leave they cost us money by carrying home the goods. They have no loyalty to us any more. That's why the Japs are ahead of us. Did you see that little Jap sucker on TV the other night? He said that America can't be good at everything all the time and that we must allow some nations to be at least pretty good at some things. I felt like pushing my fist right through the TV and mashing in that little Jap's face. Boy, was he rubbing it in. Reagan will take care of them. The Japs and Iranians, the blacks and all the rest."

"A fine fellow. He has a closet full of Levi Strauss jeans. They got him on the cover of *Hour-Glass* magazine in a blue denim shirt. He'll help the industry. He's a sharp dresser and well-groomed. Every sixteen days he gets a haircut."

"That issue of *Hour-Glass* isn't even out. How did you know all of that?"

"There's this kid down in hardware. His name is Oswald Zumwalt. He has some great ideas. His wife is a copy editor at *Hour-Glass*. She gets advance copies. He's always bringing me copies of *Hour-Glass* before it reaches the stands. I like the kid. He's very ambitious. He's inviting me over for dinner, later this afternoon. You know, since Grace died, I haven't gone out so much. It's nice to have someone make dinner for you. Anyway, Zumwalt says that we could cut costs if the whole industry got behind one Santa Claus and made this Santa Claus available only to those who could pay. We would charge people admission to come into the stores and have their kids consult Santa Claus. He said that Santa Claus is too dispersed as it is. Zumwalt's very smart. Hyperkinetic, but smart. He says we could cut down on labor costs by doing what the Japanese do."

"What do the Japs do?"

"Hire robots. He says that in Japan the robots work alongside humans so that the humans have to work harder to keep up. He says that they already have robots who can take over from the models."

"The women would never go for that. They want flesh and blood, ass and tits."

"They can create women. You ever see that film, *The Stepford Wives*? Well, in this film there's this mad professor in a New England town who is turning all of these women into robots. All of them pushing shopping carts, smiling, behaving themselves. You couldn't tell the difference."

"I see what you mean, Herman." Cinderella in a low-cleavaged gown danced on a float with her Prince Charming. The float was shaped like a castle. The two men stared.

"Maybe you ought to give this Zumwalt kid a promotion. See what he's got. Rare to find a kid who's ambitious these days. I think Reagan's going to bring back the sixties. I don't want to go through that again. Cities burned. Insurance rates shooting sky high."

"He cooks, too. He's cooking dinner today."

"What's the matter with him?"

"Plenty of fellows do that these days. Cook, babysit."

"How's your son doing?"

"He's still in the seminary. I got a card from him. It was covered with strange-looking stamps."

"Yeah, what did he have to say?"

"He said he was having some kind of dispute with his superiors. He said they were too devoted to orthodoxy and ritual. He claims that he's a part of a new church. A church devoted to social and political issues. His position was the source of his troubles."

"That's a mouthful. My nephew always did have a head on his shoulders."

"There's something that worries me, though, George."

"What's that, Herman?"

"When he came home for the holidays he brought this strange man with him called Brother Andrew. This Andrew kept addressing my kid as Bishop. He kept referring to him as the Bishop this and the Bishop that. He wouldn't call my kid by his right name. My son ain't no Bishop. I'm wondering what the hell is going on." A float passes by carrying Dean Clift, the top male model of the United States. He is modeling some snug-fitting jeans. Men and women struggle with the police. They want to touch him, to feel him. There are a few anxious moments as they almost turn the float over.

Look at them. They'd cut out my heart if I'd let them. Take parts of it home as souvenirs. I have dreams of their fanglike eyes staring at me. My public. My audience. My life. When I'm in bed at night I see hands reaching through the walls, trying to get me. Will they always crave this body? This body which has never shown an inch of flab. It's becoming more difficult to keep this body in shape. Maybe I should think of a new career. Sometimes I can't distinguish between the real me and the billboard me. My life's story seems to be a series of billboards, television commercials, beer ads, cigarette ads, shirt ads. I live between the covers of magazines like the commercial Buster Brown who lived in a shoe.

The crowd surges once again to get their grips on Mr. Dean Clift. The whole country wanted to cling to him, to become treacly over him. It had been a pretty easy life except for the tragedy occurring a few years before, and now there were muscle spasms, and palpitations, backaches, and sometimes on cold mornings he couldn't move his index finger.

Soon I will look like Santa Claus, and what then? If Elizabeth hadn't made those wise investments there would be no future for me at all. She manages the house on the Hudson and the apartment in New York. But what good is it? The city is overflowing with bag people, trash people, beggars of all kinds, refugees. Maybe I should accept those politicians' offers. Run for Congress from the silk stocking district. Looks easy being a congressman. You don't even have to show up for work half the time. You meet interesting people and get to travel a lot. Something to think about.

They have to speed up Dean Clift's float. Some of the crowd has pushed through the barricade and have to be clubbed by the police.

"Handsome fellow, huh, George? He looks like Steve Canyon. That set square jaw and those comic-book blue eyes."

"He isn't queer, is he?" asked Herman.

"Naw. He's married and he's got two kids. Well, one kid now. A girl. The oldest kid was killed in a bizarre accident at Harvard. He was trying to hoist a Confederate flag over his fraternity house and this other kid, a campus radical, started wrestling with him and the kid fell. He was impaled on a spike and was carried off wriggling on that spike. They had to cut off part of the fence to take him away to the hospital. He was dead on arrival. The kid that did it got away. He dropped out of sight."

"How awful. Did you hear the news?"

"No, what news?"

"They're thinking about running Clift for Congress from the silk stocking district."

"What?"

"But he doesn't know anything about anything. I've never heard him express a thought. At the parties, he's always smiling at you, flashbulbs popping, beautiful women on each arm, the hostesses outdoing themselves to see that he gets what he wants."

"Yeah, but he's not just a jock. He does more than lift weights. He's the highest-paid model in the United States. His face is everywhere. He gets as much as twenty thousand an hour. If a man like that had a brain he'd be dangerous. He's got his wife managing his investments, according to an interview I read in *Women's Wear Daily*. Calls her Mommy. Mommy this, Mommy that. Totally dependent on her. She packs his clothes and draws his bath water. A shrewd woman, though. Besides, who knows, they may become so cautious they won't even want an actor fronting for them. He may pull a Mr. Smith on them."

"What do you mean?"

"That movie. *Mr. Smith Goes to Washington*. In this one scene, Mr. Smith gets up and makes a speech in Congress in which he exposes all of the corruption in the land, and this one Senator, played by Claude Rains, becomes so agitated he leaps to his feet and confesses it all. I have a cousin who puts it this way: a dancer's greatest fear is losing his legs, a painter's his vision; an actor sometimes forgets where the real him ends and the character takes over. Writers too. You know, this guy Simenon, he said he quit writing because his characters began to dominate him, tell him what to do. So just like in *Mr. Smith Goes to Washington*, the actor may tear up the script, ignore the teleprompter, and really say what's on his mind. They might decide to replace him with a robot."

"Aw, George, things will never get that bad."

"Don't count on it. A university in Santa Monica is working on a doll that will be so real it will be macabre. They plan to have it on the market by Christmas 'eighty-four."

The men chuckle. "What do you say we go over to the club for a drink? I'm tired of the parade."

"I can only stay for one martini. I have to fly to Texas

tomorrow. Are they going to be sore when they see the bad sales figures."

"Yeah, it must be tough on you, Herman. Arguing before those Texans. These slumps occur, but business ought to pick up. You'd think they'd give us more time."

"What do they know about time? All they know is money and filthy bathroom humor."

"We should have never sold Rehab Oil those shares. They know absolutely nothing about the department store business. Our grandfather comes over here from Germany. Builds the store from a pushcart peddling pots and pans. And then we modernize it and bring it into the twentieth century with high class merchandise, but how could we compete with these big merchandise chains and their discounts and their computers and space-age marketing techniques?"

"Maybe we're done for, George. Maybe they'll get rid of us and bring in some younger blood, some anonymous clean-shaven face who'll do their bidding. The East is dying. We're dying. Everything is shifting to the West. The sunbelt, and the gold coast of California. The Japs have bought up about three states in the West."

"The East will never die. The East will suffer some setbacks, but it won't die. Too much sun out there. Genius thrives in bad weather."

The first boss signaled the driver. The huge fossil-fuels monster turned from the parade barricades and slowly headed towards the East Side. As it moved away, Sister Sledge rode by on a float shaped like a huge turkey.

Vixen, standing near the curb, knew about Sister Sledge. She remembered their song, "We Are Family," the theme song of the Pittsburgh Pirates. "We Are Family." It never occurred to her that it was sung in march time. She wished she and her husband, Sam, were a family. They were drifting apart. During the holidays, she began to yearn for the old values. Of home and hearth. Maybe it was her New England background. The

white steeples, the cemeteries, and the fir trees of New
Hampshire and the white birch of Vermont. She'd cooked a
Thanksgiving feast for herself and Sam. Turkey, corn,
pumpkin pie. That's how much the holidays got to her. She
would always get the blues during the holidays. But Sam hadn't
come home. He had said he was going down to one of the East
Side piers to hear a jazz concert, but he hadn't returned.
Maybe there was another woman. She caught him once with
another woman and he said that he had to do it because the
creative drive is connected to the libido and that he had a
painter's block. She wondered was he fucking that dark-haired
slinky-looking waitress down on Prince Street. She wondered if
he knew she was fucking Romeo, his best friend. Unlike Sam,
who sometimes made her feel like a human doughnut, Romeo
took his time. He looked like Julius LaRosa and did it elegant
like Marcello Mastroianni.

This marriage was the pits. She was tired of the painters
coming over to her house, smoking pot and drinking beer and
referring to painters who weren't present as prostitutes and
faggots. She wanted to have Sam's baby but he'd smoked so
much dope that his sperm, instead of containing the population of a small town, held that of a bus stop in Oakland. Plus,
he had a chronic cough now. She'd read that marijuana
contained some kind of fungus similar to that one finds in the
damp dark corners of a house. She was tired of working as a
busgirl and ticket taker while he painted. She was better
educated than his friends were and if they'd listen to her she
could tell them why nobody would give them a show. The stuff
they were heralding as new was done thirty years ago in
Belgium. She was tired of New York. She didn't have any
girlfriends she could relate to. New York was grimy and the sky
always had the color of an embalmed oyster. In her elevator,
they'd found a woman who had been brutally raped and
murdered; she had been stabbed thirty-two times. Drunks
urinated at the entrance to their loft. They were three months

behind in their rent because Sam had quit his shipping-clerk
job in order to, as he put it, devote full time to his "art." He
was in bad shape. He wouldn't even clean underneath his
nails. He was always scratching his scalp. He gave her the
crabs, and his belly was beginning to drop over his belt, and all
he did was lie around or talk a lot of feverish incoherent
meaningless jargon full of "O Wow." He used to say "heavy" a
lot but he met a French painter at a party and now he was
saying *formidable* a lot. She was having fun today watching the
Macy's parade.

The parade looked like an illustration by a well-known
American illustrator who smoked a pipe and owned a prominent Adam's apple. Melba Moore sang atop a float sponsored
by the *Daily News*. It was made of a miniature skyline of New
York dominated by a huge apple. Melba sat on the apple
singing "I Love New York."

Sam's friends would ridicule Vixen for taking delight in
this Thanksgiving Day Parade. She was wearing the same black
bear coat she'd worn in college. She had blown hair. Her hands
were shoved into her pockets. She had a feeling of well-being
because she was close to a decision. She always had this feeling
when her mind was being made up and she was about to take
another step. She'd been dreaming of her father recently. He'd
died of a heart attack a few years ago. Her mother was smart
and glamorous and didn't have much time to be a mother.
She'd run away to New Mexico and, when last heard, she was
drinking herself to death.

Her friend Jennifer had moved to Alaska. Jennifer had
written that there were lots of jobs and men available in Alaska.
A poet, Ed Dorn, had said that Alaska reminded him of Raquel
Welch. She wondered what he meant by that. Perhaps one day
she would find out.

The Rockettes marched by. They towed a swan-shaped
sleigh whose passenger was none other than Santa Claus

himself. He was waving and wishing everybody a Happy Thanksgiving and a Merry Christmas.

3

One of the marching bands was so loud that Bob Krantz asked his secretary to close the window. He is seated in his office at Whyte B.C. busily conversing through a custard-colored pushbutton telephone with his boss, the network's owner, James Whyte. "I'm sorry, Mr. Whyte, but I had to close the window. They're making a big racket downstairs. The Macy's Thanksgiving Day Parade, you know. As I was saying, Mr. Whyte, you won't have to worry about Reverend Jones and those Texans. When '20 Minutes,' our newsmagazine, finishes with him, his name won't be worth a hamper full of dirty underwear."

"His direct-mail campaign against violence and homosexuality on television is worrying our sponsors. What do you plan to do about it?" boomed the patrician voice on the other end of the phone.

"We have some leaks from the I.R.S. As soon as they finish with the Reverend, he'll be put away for about ten years."

"You don't say." Krantz could hear Mr. Whyte's broad smile on the other end. "You have the goods on him. Good fellow, Krantz, good fellow."

"I knew I had to protect my tush, Mr. Whyte. I anticipated that the fundamentalists would be upset with our new lineup and so I have enough evidence, about forty pounds, to close down Jones's empire for a long time."

"How are the inauguration plans coming?"

"We plan to have live coverage from the time the President-elect and first lady greet the Carters on the steps of the White House until the last of the eight balls is over."

"I'll tell the President-elect. His friends are shelling out eight million dollars for this thing and the taxpayers are contributing four. It should be quite a show. Quite a show. There will be Marine Guards standing at attention all over the place."

"When you see the President, will you do me a favor, sir?"

"What's that, Krantz?"

"Would you tell him to go easy on the makeup? One night he came on the tube and he resembled one of Count Dracula's wives, he was wearing so much paint. And tell him, if you will, sir, to avoid as many right profiles as possible. His right jaw? Shadows hang there. It looks like the entrance to a lagoon."

"Krantz, you sound as if you don't approve of the President. What's eating you?"

"O, no, no. I want to make the President look good. Why, it was me who directed the cameramen to do full shots of him during the debates. That way he looked big, commanding, superhuman. It feels good to be a white man again with him in office. One hour after the election results were known, we made all the black employees get rid of the cornrow hairstyles. I'm mellowing, Mr. Whyte. I've come a long way from S.D.S. and Woodstock. Why, this morning I went out and bought some cowboy boots."

"Cowboy boots, huh. Krantz, how do you think I'd look in some of those boots?"

"You'd look fine, Mr. Whyte."

"Then why don't you order some for me. Have them put some spurs on them."

"I certainly will, Mr. Whyte. It's as good as done."

"Who do you think is going to win that game?"

"I think the Raiders might give Philadelphia a hard time.

They might even win. Oakland has a good team, but if they can penetrate the Philadelphia defense, who knows? They might even win by two touchdowns."

"You might have a point, Krantz. Send me over some more of that stuff you brought to the party."

"What stuff, Mr. Whyte?"

"That white dustlike substance. You remember how when some was spilled on the rug everybody got down on all fours and sniffed the rug. It was so pleasant. You referred to it as snow, I believe."

"Certainly will bring some, Mr. Whyte. Which hotel are you going to be staying in during the inaugural?"

"The Hilton."

"I'll contact you there, Mr. Whyte. And again, don't worry about Reverend Jones. After our exposé he'll be back in Texas selling chili on the porch in his bare feet." Krantz puts down the phone. Opens a bottle and gulps down some pills. The room is full of teddy bears. Everywhere you look there are teddy bears. Teddy bears of all colors and sizes. Teddy bears from all over the world, but mostly from Formosa. Krantz unscrews the small navy-blue velvet teddy bear on his desk, and dips in a tiny golden spoon. He sniffs the spoon and immediately assumes an expression of exuberance. Momentarily, he feels like a genius. He is a genius. He presses a button which sets off an electric train. The train begins to circle his desk on its tiny tracks. He picks up the phone. "Jane, tell everybody I've gone down to the health club to play some racquetball."

"He's here. He's been sitting in that chair for an hour now. Ever since you got on the phone with Mr. Whyte."

"Does he seem mad?"

"He's pretty mad, and won't go away."

A robust, muscular, and well-tanned looking Rex Stuart wearing dark glasses strides vigorously into Bob Krantz's office. He has a head of silver hair and with a mustache he would look like Caesar Romero. Bob Krantz rises to extend his hand. It is doing a St. Vitus. The man angrily slams a copy of *TV Guide* onto Krantz's desk.

"Look fella, don't get nervous," Krantz says.

"I had to read about it in the *TV Guide!*" He is furious.

"I don't know what you're driving at," Krantz says, weakly.

"Don't play innocent with me."

"Hey, calm down. It wasn't my decision, it was Mr. Whyte's, he decided to cut your part."

"Cut my part. Look, you little turd, I *made* 'Sorrows and Trials.' Millions of people wouldn't even watch it if it weren't for my part."

"You're wrong about that." Bob Krantz removes some papers from a folder on his desk. "Remember when you were out for two weeks a few months ago?"

"Yeah, what about it?"

"The ratings for 'Sorrows and Trials' went up eight percent. And O, yeah, where did you say you went during those two weeks?"

"My aunt died in Philadelphia. I had to settle the estate."

"O, yeah, then what are these?" He shoved the Xeroxes of the man's bills from Pleasant Grove Manor, an alcoholic rehabilitation hospital about thirty miles from L.A.

"Where did you get those?"

"I don't have to tell you where I got nothin', you fuck. Let's face it, fella, you're a has-been. You're slipping. You're rusty with your cue cards. I've seen it happen to old guys like you. They lose their reflexes. All of those takes we do of your scenes cost us money. We overlooked that, but then Mr. Whyte was driving through the gates and he passed that picket line you and your buddies set up."

"So that's it. You slime. You're still mad about the settlement. Ninety-five percent of the people in this industry make less than five thousand dollars per year and you'd begrudge them a share of the royalties from cable television.

Five thousand dollars; why, you spend more than that on these goddamned trains." The man kicks a few tiny boxcars across the room.

"Hey, what the hell's wrong with you?" Krantz says, diving for the trains. "You'll pay for this. You'll pay," Krantz says, gathering up the boxcars, one of which had been broken in half.

"Like a fucking two-year-old, playing with trains and teddy bears."

"Get out. Get out." The man walks over to where Krantz is bent down on the floor, gives him a hard kick in the rear, and leaves the room. Krantz screams in the background. The man walks toward the elevator through the curious who have left their offices to see what has happened. Outside the building, he looks up and down for his limousine; it is nowhere in sight. He buttons his sports jacket and turns to the black doorman who stands in front of the building. The doorman was examining Stuart's white slacks and white shoes. "Your driver went to the airport," the man says, stroking his chin.

"He what?" Krantz's attacker says.

"He had to pick up the guy they flew in from New York to take your place. Your driver said you wouldn't be needing him anymore," the doorman says, smirking.

"Well, call me a cab."

"Call one yourself. There's a pay phone in the lobby." The former star of "Sorrows and Trials" turns around. He looks up. The curious are staring at him from their windows. He reaches into his pockets for a dime and goes into the lobby.

4

Only children and Mr. Dean Clift could get by on their good looks. You watched as in the distance, sirens screaming, Dean Clift, the model, who stopped the parade, was whisked away but not even this took your attention away from the little black man with rough-looking red hair and his dummy. Your two-year-old was watching the man with intense fascination. The little black devil even stared at your little Freddie Jr. The little man wore black glasses, flawless white suit and white shoes. He had set up an elegant little stand covered with cloth upon which had been sewn a portrait of the late Emperor Haile Selassie. He was telling the crowd that he could do an imitation of any famous world leader they knew. While he was working the crowd, drawing attention away from the parade, his little dummy was also making a pitch. The little dummy was black, owned red lips, and wore a sinister fixed smile. The ventriloquist kept referring to the dummy as baldhead. He even called the crowd baldheads though most of them possessed hair. There was quite a bit of cash atop the ventriloquist's stand. The little dummy was waging some card bets in a game of three-card monte. It held three cards, two red and one black. Every time you hit black the dummy paid you, but when you hit red, you paid the dummy. The dummy kept saying red you win, black you lose, and as he slapped the cards on the table, he'd say red, black, red, black, and then in reverse, black, red, black, red, black, red. Then, as if this scene weren't outrageous enough, the little dummy's goat was up on its hind legs dancing to a Reggae version of "Santa Claus is coming tonight," but the lyrics had been changed, and instead of saying "Santa," they sang what sounded like "Santy." Santy Claus. In a minor, mournful key. Your child doesn't want to leave but the tinny, shrill music, coming from the little man's primitive sound system aided by two egg crates, was becoming annoying.

The two-year-old was screaming, and some of the adults in the parade crowd cast suspicious glances your way. He was screaming so loud it seems that he drowns out the trombones. You decide to slip into a restaurant on the parade route to buy him some ice cream. This usually shuts him up. He throws tantrums until he gets what he wants. You'd like to whack him good across his bottom but your wife is reading childrearing books which advise against this. They counsel patience.

As the child grows he tells you things. He tells you about nations and individuals. About how civilizations come into being. You're glad that two-year-olds don't have access to ICBMs the way the responsible leaders in your government do.

You're forty years old and a third-class citizen in your own home. Everything he wants he gets. You fight in court all day and when you come home you want a gin fizz. You want to relax with the *New York Post*. You read the *Times* in the morning. Sometimes the pages are torn and scattered about the room. The two-year-old has something against the newspapers because when people are concentrating on long white sheets nobody pays any attention to him. He says no to everything. Take a bath. No. Eat dinner. No. Go to bed. No. The terrible twos are twins to the terrible nos. When you go out with your wife, she insists on taking him with you. You still remember the night in the French restaurant when he threw the veal and sauce to the floor, and set fire to the waitress's hair with the lit candle. You settled with the waitress out of court. And every time the serenaders sang their French country songs, he'd scream and ask to go to the bathroom and when you got into the bathroom he didn't have to go.

Human beings at two harbor cravings that have to be immediately quenched, demand things, and if another human being of their size and age enters the picture, there's war. Human beings at two have to be read to, pampered, and assisted in their toilet. Every two-year-old is an emperor or an empress. Walking with him on the parade route has its advantages. The little tot liked the clowns. He smiled his most engaging smile when he saw the float of Bullwinkle the Moose and Rocky the Flying Squirrel pass by. Some women commented on how cute he looks. He gets his hair mussed, and you get phone numbers. The woman who said she'd come to your Greenwich Village office next week says she'll bring quiche and wine. It's a two-story building with a spiraling staircase. It looks like a French publishing house on Rue Jacob: Count, Earl, and King.

You're making progress. You're moving up in the world. One day, you'll have an office on Park Avenue. One day. Before the kid finally breaks down, you were able to catch some scenes from Broadway shows. *The Pirates of Penzance. Barnum. One Mo' Time.* The Jamaican dancers are great. You wish you could take the wife and the kid to Jamaica, but you've heard that things have gotten very racial down there. That whites like you have been molested and there have even been a couple of machete murders.

You can't even get to the beach these days without wading through politics. Politics. God, if anyone told you ten years ago that you'd be voting for Reagan you would have doubled over in laughter. He used to be funny like his friend the 1930s peach picker, Roy Rogers. Hilarious. What did he say? When Trigger died he had them stuff Trigger and mount Trigger, and when he dies he wants them to stuff him and put him on Trigger. The waitress scowls at you as she takes the order for three scoops of ice cream. Americans are edgy these days. Dissatis-

fied. Carter talked about a malaise, French for "the blues."
The kid points out the scoops he wants. Yuk. "Boola Boola
Moola Marble," "Goodbye Mr. Chips," and "Manila Vanilla." Another thing about two-year-olds. They have very bad
taste. They make Liberace seem subdued. He's quiet now,
busily licking the ice cream which will soon melt on his sticky
hands, if a scoop or two doesn't fall to the floor first. But wait.
The fellow sitting there at the counter. Nance Saturday. He
was the brightest guy in law school class. Then, he shocked
everybody by dropping out. Looks like he's been out playing
tennis. The seaman's hat, calf-length white socks with red and
blue stripes at the top, sneakers, shorts, and windbreaker. Still
has that thick mustache and is wearing those glasses. He used
to get a lot of kidding about those glasses. He looks up from the
newspaper and notices you. He smiles. You take the kid in tow
and approach him. "Hey, Nance Saturday." He looks up.
"Don't you recognize me?"

"Yeah, I recognize you. We were in the same class at
Rutgers." He doesn't seem to be very thrilled. "Your kid?"

"Yeah, did I just have a scare! There was this fellow, a
little black fellow down the street who looked as if he had a red
lion's mane covering his head, and he was smoking a
marijuana cigarette that was as huge as a morning glory."

"I think they call them locks."

"The fellow was a ventriloquist. He could talk at the same
time as his little dummy who was engaging the crowd in a
game of three-card monte. He said that he was a descendant of
a slave named Pompey, a master ventriloquist of the Old South
who escaped from slavery by throwing his voice. I've never seen
anything like it. He could talk and puff on a marijuana
cigarette, imitating President Eisenhower, Winston Churchill,
and other famous world leaders. He said that although he was
an ordinary, insignificant, and barely literate speaker, he was
fortunate that someone named Jah made it possible for the
Emperor to speak through him."

"Risto Rasta."

"What do you mean?"

"You know, with all of this Reggae music and carrying on, every con artist on Forty-second Street is trying to use the Reggae scam to get over."

"O, is that it? The fellow was drawing quite a crowd. He was diverting attention from the Macy's parade, which takes some doing.

"Been a long time, Nance. How've you been getting along?"

"Chasing down hunches and turning up clues at the moment." People couldn't get over Nance. He had one of those thick, handlebar mustaches. He could have been a member of Queen Elizabeth's guard with that mustache, a reader of Kipling and an imbiber of gin from a bottle with Queen Victoria's picture on it. You couldn't read his face because he had a dark face and this disturbed people. What was really disturbing was his eyes from Kung-Fu-Tse. They didn't call him Nance for nothing. He didn't have to go out and get it; it usually came to him.

"Where you living, Nance?"

"I have an apartment in Chelsea."

"Did you marry?"

"Yeah, for a year or so. I don't blame her for leaving. She wanted to be independent. She felt that she was drawn into my orbit. The funny thing is that we can't seem to get around to obtaining a divorce. She says she can't seem to get out of my pull. You might know her—Virginia, Virginia Saturday—you might have seen her on television."

"I think I have. She does that interview show on Channel seven, doesn't she? My wife and I watch it every night. Swell-looking gal. Her interview with Giscard D'Estaing was super.

"We live out in Staten Island now. I have a law office down in the Village. You know, Nance, never did understand why you didn't finish law school. You were at the top of the class. Why did you drop out?"

"There's no law in this country. Only power and class—"

"Too bad about this Reagan fellow. It's going to be bad on black people, huh?"

"The perfect phony."

"Well, I've heard that he's pretty tough, but nobody ever said anything about the guy being a phony. Sounds like a lot of inflammatory Mau Mau rhetoric to me. Look, Nance, black people aren't interesting any more. They've become dull and are not as exciting as they used to be. There are just too many other things for us to be concerned with than helping them all the time. A lot of people see it Reagan's way. Things have got to change in this country, Nance. Reagan's the man."

"Well spoken, Eliot Ness. But his name is not Reagan, it's O'Regan. He's Irish, yet he's always calling himself Anglo. I don't trust a man who identifies with the people who've kept the Irish in bondage for eight hundred years. He's passing for white."

"Yeah, well, look, Nance, it's nice seeing you. Come down for a drink sometime. Here's my card." You give him your card. Hey, where's the kid? The waitress smiles and points to the private banquet facilities in the rear. But you can see the spots of ice cream on the carpet that lead to that room. You see flakes of the cone which have already been crushed under someone's heel. You open the door and are confronted with rows of what appear to be white cabbages underneath chandeliers. These turn out to be hair styles. Some elderly women are seated, having a big Thanksgiving spread, and in the middle of the setting, like he owned the place, is your son, chocolate pudding all over his chin and mouth. Somebody has given him a Spiderman comic. The women smile. A lady turns to you. "Is this your child? He's so sweet. So well-mannered. So delightful. You must be a good father." And the child gives you such a look of innocence, you can't imagine what got into him. Things get into two-year-olds. Sour one second, sweet the next. Demanding. You don't have to live with him twenty-four hours a day, lady, you start to say, but instead you smile and reach for his hand and lead him out of the restaurant. Two-year-olds.

In mankind's mirific misty past they were sacrificed to the winter gods. Maybe that's why some gods act so young. Ogun, so childish that he slays both the slavemaster and the slave.

Two-year-olds are what the id would look like if the id could ride a tricycle. That's the innocent side of two, but the terrible side as well. A terrible world the world of two-year-olds. The world of the witch's door you knock on when your mother told you not to go near the forest in the first place. Pigs building houses of straw. Vain and egotistic gingerbread men who end up riding on the nose of a fox. Nightmares in the closet. Someone is constantly trying to eat them up. The gods of winter crave them—the gods of winter who, some say, are represented by the white horse that Saint Nicholas, or Saint Nick, rides as he enters Amsterdam, his blackamoor servant, Peter, following with his bag of switches and candy. Two-year-olds are constantly looking over their shoulders for the man in the shadows carrying the bag. Black Peter used to carry them across the border into Spain.

Fred King took his son's hand and walked out of the restaurant. He glanced back and caught Nance Saturday, drinking coffee and examining some maps that were spread out on the table in front of him.

5

Oswald Zumwalt lifted the pot's lid and dipped the ladle into the steaming hot pea soup. He opened the oven door and examined the turkey which was beginning to turn brown. The rice was becoming fluffy. He was about to prepare a salad when Jane walked in. She was what they called in the old days "a diminutive brunette." She removed her coat, opened the refrigerator door, and poured herself a tall glass of grapefruit juice.

"Smells good."

"O, hi, dear." Zumwalt looked up and then returned to his chores. She noticed the third plate.

"Are we having someone for dinner?" she asked.

"The boss," he said. "You know, since his wife died he's been a lonely man." She made a face. "I hope you don't mind."

"You know how I feel about your boss. I'm with the Alternative Christmas group. You've read our pamphlets. Schneider Brothers' department store has a long history of discrimination against women and minorities. They hustle those awful war toys. We threw up a boycott there last Christmas. Don't you remember?" He placed her hand on his shoulder. She brushed it off. He smelled something burning. The rolls. He rushed to the oven and removed some of them. He forgot to use a potholder and burned his hand. He shook his hand and then ran into the living room where Jane sat on the couch tapping her foot and pouting. The other furniture included a butterfly chair, a blue director's chair, and book shelves. Three books lay on the coffee table: Abbie Hoffman's *Soon to be a Major Motion Picture*; *The Third Wave*, by Alvin Toffler; and Richard Brautigan's *Dreaming of Babylon*. A roach from a marijuana cigarette lay in an ashtray. Zumwalt noticed it and removed it before pleading with his wife.

"I thought we were going to have this Christmas alone," she said. Her Levi's fitted well, and she wore a blouse which was royally laced. Smith, '76.

"We have enough. Look, it's not every day that the boss takes a fellow's offer for dinner." Zumwalt had the head of a baby chick, especially around the nose. "Hey, what happened to your hair?"

"Thought I'd get a haircut." She notices the small, gray Christmas tree.

"Cheerful, isn't it," he says, noticing her eyes glancing in that direction.

"What the fuck is going on?" she said. "We've never had a tree."

"I bought it because—well, I haven't had one in the house for years. I guess I'm becoming nostalgic."

"Nostalgic, my ass; you're trying to impress the boss. You've gotten hung up on that fucking job. This was supposed to be a stop on the way to Montana. We were going to save some money and then go to Montana. You promised. You took that stupid job at the department store and I went to work as a copy editor for *Hour-Glass*."

He sat down next to her and took her hand. "But don't you see how unrealistic that is? Montana. What would I do in Montana? Break horses? It was just one of our silly dreams."

"Silly dreams, he calls them. So that's what our relationship has been, silly dreams. You've changed, Ziggie. Monopoly capitalism is still on the march. Wasting the world.

Oppressing the underclass. Remember we were going to take the fight to the West, all of our friends."

"I'm thirty-two years old; I can't go around playing at rebellion." The kitchen. He rose and dashed into the kitchen. The rice was sticking to a burnt pan. It had turned brown. She followed him.

"O, shit. See what you made me do. Look, I don't want to discuss it any more. It's time for me to get serious. Over at the department store they listen to me. I have a future there."

"So they got you."

"What do you mean?"

"The manure heap. From now on your life will be measured in terms of profit and loss. Well, I'm not going to be a nine-to-five copy editor for the rest of my life. I'm tired of the East. It stinks here. All of the contradictions of the capitalistic system are in plain view. The pitiful vagrants and the limousines with their shades drawn, the fascist impersonal skyscrapers. Hideous glass boxes. I haven't seen a bird or a wild tree in so long I forget what they look like. And then, suppose they find you. Then what? You'll go to jail. For what you did, you might even be shot on sight. Suppose the plastic surgeon squeals."

"I'm tired of running. I'll just have to take my chances. I have a future in the department store business, and I'm not going to blow it. For the first time in my life I'm making my own decisions on how to run my life, and I'm not a dutiful imbecile doing what you, my parents, or some nutty left-wing organization wants me to do."

"Man, are you into a power thing." The buzzer rings.

"That's him now." Zumwalt embraced his wife. "Look, hon, please try to be civil. He's an old and lonely guy. He and his brother both. If his brother hadn't had to leave for Texas, I would have invited him too." She smiles. "And don't bring up that alternative Christmas junk either. He hates that shit." Jane frowned.

*   *   *

Ebenezer Scrooge bahed and humbugged his way through the 1980 Christmas. A cold wave, a bitter season indeed; the icebreakers were kept very busy. In Florida, oranges and grapefruit perished. And around January the omen-watchers began to look for signs. They knew that JFK was doomed when Robert Frost read his inaugural poem, "The Gift Outright," condemning Indian culture. The lectern caught fire. Nixon? Nixon's goose was cooked when he dropped the first baseball of the season.

On January 17th, two workers preparing the bleachers for the fortieth President's inaugural fell when the scaffolding collapsed. One man was killed, the other seriously injured.

It was a season of dry winds and biting snow. Scrooge's winter, "as mean as a junkyard dog." Giant (fifty-inch wingspan) Snowy Arctic Owls landed on eastern rooftops and the newspapers said that they rarely traveled that far south.

Not only was it the coldest in forty years, but it was the longest Christmas ever. In keeping with Jimmy Carter's pledge that the White House Christmas tree be unlit until the American hostages held by Iran were released, the tree was finally lit on the night of January 20th. On that day, bells rang in New York City, and the hallelujah chorus was heard, throughout the land, for many days afterwards.

A Future
Christmas

6

Winter is the mummer's season because it covers the earth with a mask. Twenty-five miles from one of Alaska's most populous cities lies a complex of buildings forming a small village. The headquarters of Oswald Zumwalt's North Pole Development Corporation. Soon, these buildings will be sold and the whole company will move its headquarters to the North Pole. That is, if Congressman Kroske can gather the necessary votes to get it out of his committee—he has assured Zumwalt that it is a cinch. Inside one of the artless, faceless buildings Vixen sits in a Danish chair. On her desk are a pile of papers, a pastry on a paper plate, and a coffee in a paper cup. Vixen's staff is putting the last touches on Santa Claus, who stands there like a mute human doll. She looks into his whipped eyes, which have so captured the heart of America. She examines his ermine jacket and his shiny black boots. Santa and his entourage are about to leave for New York via Seattle, where they will rendezvous with Oswald Zumwalt and some of the staff already there. Vixen was tired. She'd gotten into an argument with her boyfriend the night before. They were always arguing.

"Everything looks ready," Vixen said to her staff. They were all bundled up for the trip. "Are there any questions?" Vixen asked. There were none. Vixen was a pro. She had caught Oswald Zumwalt's eye when she first came to work for North Pole Development Corporation, shortly after arriving in Alaska from New York.

Outside, Santa rode with his German helper, Blitz, in the lead limousine which was followed by campers and a bus carrying some of the Alaska press people. The winter sun was up and shining. It was a radiant day, the last Saturday in November. A charter flight would take him and his party to New York. They would spend the rest of the day greeting department store executives, toy manufacturers, before their grand welcome to New York City, marking the official beginning of the Christmas season. The van moved towards the airport. The bars along the street were empty. Some of the store windows had been smashed.

"Where are the Indians, Blitz?"

"O, didn't you hear, sir?"

"No, what happened?"

"The Indians tore the place up last night. Something about a sacred spruce they wanted to save. The government wants to take it. Some old chief is keeping the lumberjacks away from it. He's placed himself between the tree and the authorities. Imagine these Indians, getting worked up over some tree." S.C. pulled out a bottle of Wild Turkey from his bag and took an ample swig. Wild Turkey, a precious, silky ointment for the soul, so precious that in Kentucky the Wild Turkey distilleries are guarded by dogs and guns.

"Would you like a taste, Blitz?" Blitz answered by reaching his hand into the back seat. Blitz loved Santa. So human. So down-to-earth despite his reputation for scaling rooftops. Everybody loved Santa.

7

"Well, where is he?" the huge gruff one said. He was a big mountainous man who gave off a fishy odor. "We ain't got all day."

"He should be arriving any minute," said Jerry, the Forest Ranger. "He'll explain what's going on. He knows them. He's part of them." The big man and three other Gussucks began loading their shotguns and putting on their bullet-proof vests.

"He'd better explain it good, because we've just about run out of patience. Downtown turning over cars and things. This thing has to come to a quick conclusion. I aim to get me some red meat tonight." The other Gussucks laughed. The door opened and in breezed Flinch Savvage, the half-breed native liaison. He wore dark green woolen socks, galoshes, and hooded coat. He removed the coat; underneath he wore gray slacks, plaid jacket, and black turtleneck sweater. He smelled like pine, was freshly shaved, and talked like Richard Burton. The Gussucks looked him up and down.

"I'm sorry I'm late. I came as quickly as I heard."

"Things look bad. The old chief won't let anybody get near that tree and Washington is calling up here for it. They've sent these men to remove the old chief. Maybe you can explain to the old chief. Maybe you can tell him that these men mean business. They've got shotguns. It's going to get worse. Today the Indians ran up and down the streets, dragging every

Gussuck driver they could get their hands on from his car. One man was stomped to death."

"Captain, you have to realize that these people embrace beliefs that are alien to your western ideas. They haven't had the advantages of a good education." The Gussucks exchanged glances; they smirked.

"Look, sonny, you'd better get that injun away from that tree before we get to him. The First Lady wants that tree. She's very finicky and always gets her way. They sent me to get that tree and I'm not leaving until I get that tree."

"Very well, I'll do my best, but I can't promise anything."

"It's up to you. They know your language. They'll listen to you."

Flinch Savvage put on his coat, left the office, and began his snowy trek into the woods, until he came upon the old medicine man. He was covered with snow. Even the hair above his eyes held snow. He was looking straight ahead. Flinch Savvage approached him and squatted.

"Look, Chief, the Gussucks are preparing to move in here to arrest you. Why don't you give it up? Why do you want to make it so hard on yourself? The young people in town are shooting up the place. They're going to bring in some real troopers. There's going to be bloodshed.

"If you move away, everything will end peacefully. Just quit now; you have nothing to gain from this."

"The tree is alive," the old man said.

"That tree is not alive. It's not a person. It's only a dead piece of wood. O, why am I trying to tell you. Why didn't I stay at Cambridge?"

Flinch Savvage rose and headed back towards the Forest Ranger's office. He entered.

"Well?" the captain asked.

"I can't do anything. It's going to be very hard to persuade them to abandon their traditions. There's nothing I can do."

"I knew we were wasting time. Let's move, men." The

captain and his men went out into the cold. They headed for the spruce tree and the old tradition-bearer.

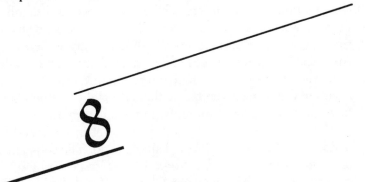

Vixen was lying next to Flinch Savvage, staring at the ceiling, sobbing. The polar-bear rug was soft under their skin. They'd just taken a bath in Vixen's black marbled sunken tub. Two glasses of red wine sat next to them.

"I'm just supposed to lie there and just let you hump up and down on me, is that what you want me to do?"

"I'm sorry, Vixen, but I can't seem to find it. It's as if your finger is being swallowed by an artichoke or something."

"You're just like all the rest of them. Nobody exists but you."

"I wasn't up to it. I had a bad day today."

"When I brought you home from the ski lodge, you were so considerate, so attracted to me. I guess you've gotten used to me."

He raised up on his elbows, reached over, and sipped from a glass of red wine.

She faced him. Ran her hand across his back. "What's wrong, Flinch?"

"Something happened today. Trouble. They tried to pull the old chief away from the tree. Old guy. Harmless fellow. But they went out there with shotguns after I failed to persuade him to move."

"O, I'm sorry, Flinch."

"He just looked at me. He said that the tree was alive. The chief reminded me of my grandfather, whose face was so full of lines it was hard to read. And those Gussucks in there, smirking, just itching for some trouble. Everywhere you Americans go, you bring death. The rivers die, the animals flee from you as they would from a fire. They know. American angels of death. Can you blame these people? Can you blame them for wanting to return to their original customs?"

"Flinch, I've had a hectic day. I'm not in the mood for politics tonight. I have a lot of planning to do. The company is preparing to move to the North Pole. Oswald Zumwalt is constructing a domed city there. Christmas Land. I'm surprised you haven't heard about it. It's been on television every night."

"I don't watch television, unless maybe the ballet or something cultural like that is on. Besides, what about us? I can't leave here unless Washington tells me."

"I don't know about us, Flinch. If Big North moves, that means I have to move. An article appeared in the *Wall Street Journal* that mentioned speculation that I might be given a vice-presidency. I can't pass up an opportunity like that. I have to look out for myself. All of my life I've depended upon men. That hasn't worked out."

"Company woman."

"Flinch," she said, putting on a blue kimono on which was sewn a white dragon, "if you're going to be rude, you can leave. You've been up here in Alaska too long. Too much missionary school. I do what I want with my life, and I'm not going to have a man offend me with his silly value judgments." A figure appeared in the doorway. Flinch covered himself with a terrycloth robe. It was one of the little servants that the company used to aid Santa Claus. Word had it that Santa and his helpers were quite fond of each other, sometimes hitting all the bars in town during the off-season. Next to their chores with Santa, they had to work a shift at the chocolate vats, stirring boiling chocolate, and once in a while one of the little men toppled into the chocolate. Nobody missed them. Their working conditions were terrible. Now that Santa had gone to New York, his favorite helper Blitz had been assigned to help Vixen with her big apartment. He mixed drinks, answered the door, and talked on the telephone. He was a badly mangled fellow who suffered from hormone growth deficiency and didn't quite have all of his chromosomes. He wore an elf's cap and baggy pants, with a rope tied about the waist. He owned a small white beard. He had overcome his defects. He could even drive a car.

Vixen looked up. "Blitz, what do you want?"

"I'm sorry to bother you, ma'am, but your car is back from the garage."

"Just as well. Would you like to go to the ski lodge for a drink, Flinch?"

"Suits me fine," said Flinch. At that, Blitz turned his back and left the room. He didn't want to be caught rudely smirking.

Flinch put on his briefs, pants, socks, and shirt in silence. He put on a heavy coat. Vixen got into a long lynx coat, over her sweater and pants. Outside, Blitz helped Vixen into the back seat of the wolf-fur-seated Lincoln. Blitz looked Flinch up and down as he held the front door for him.

It was cold and frosty. They were dining in a restaurant which was lit up like an interrogation room.

Joe Baby was dressed, flamboyantly. He was wearing snake-skinned red cowboy boots, a mink coat, and a mink-brimmed hat. His partner, Big Meat, was got up the same way. He was Joe Baby's shadow. They lived together. They sat across from a short man who weighed three hundred pounds. He'd just polished off some white "country fresh" eggs, five slices of Virginia ham, nine pieces of whole wheat toast, and three cups of orange juice, and he was waiting for a New York steak. Joe Baby was coughing. He pulled out a white handkerchief and sneezed some phlegm into it. Big Meat took out his pills and counted three for Joe Baby, who gulped them down.

"Don't you ever stop eating?" Joe Baby asked Snow Man. Joe Baby touched the rim of his glasses.

"Thin people are the ones who die in an emergency," the Snow Man said. "They don't have any reserve," he said, after chewing on some ham. "Suppose a famine occurs. I have enough energy to see me through. You guys wouldn't last a week." Snow Man had arctic blue eyes. Under his overcoat he wore a conservative suit and striped bow tie.

"Hey, man. I don't think that be too cool. Joe Baby just got out of the hospital."

"Don't tangle with him, Meat. He'll blow your brains out and think nothing of it. That is if he can't bump you against the ceiling like a pancake. I saw him sit on a dude. It was like a steamroller rolling over on somebody." Joe Baby began to cough in such spasms that patrons at other tables turned around and stared.

"Do we deal or not," Snow Man said.

"Too steep."

"Ten thou is not steep, my friend," the Snow Man said, staring blankly at Joe Baby, who was sitting across from him. "You're asking me to drop a Bishop."

"Give him the money, Meat." The black man sitting next to Joe Baby had enough grease in his hair to fry a catfish. Some of the grease spotted the collar of his camel-haired coat and his white silk scarf. He took out a white box tied with a red ribbon and slid it towards the Snow Man.

"I'll bring you his head in a box," Snow Man said. "Gift wrapped."

"You'd better," Joe Baby said. Big Meat smiled. He took out his comb and styled his hair. The two left Snow Man in the restaurant. Outside, they climbed into an old black Cadillac Seville limousine and drove off.

Snow Man looked down at the newspaper as he took in mouthful after mouthful. There had been huge headlines for weeks. The Soviet Union was putting down rebellions in Estonia, Latvia, and the Ukraine. The rebellions that had begun in Riga had spread. Its ally, the United States, was having its share of bad luck too. Things had come to a head between the United States and an African power of unpredictable motives. The government claimed that the President was in constant consultation with his aides. At the end of the week, the Secretary of Defense was found dead, a possible suicide.

On the editorial page, there was a letter to the editor. It was one of many letters which had been coming in for five years, complaining about a decision handed down in a California court awarding exclusive rights to Santa Claus to Oswald Zumwalt's North Pole Development Corporation.

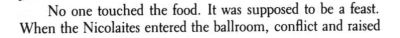

No one touched the food. It was supposed to be a feast. When the Nicolaites entered the ballroom, conflict and raised voices had immediately begun. Bro. Peter, as he was demanding to be called these days, had removed the face of Saint Nicholas from a painting above the fireplace and replaced it with one of Haile Selassie. Boy Bishop's followers objected and were threatening to summon him back from Boston, where he'd gone to officiate at the wedding of a rich patron. They were being jeered by those Nicolaites who were loyal to Bro. Peter. The Nicolaites were split down the middle.

Black Peter had been left in charge by Boy Bishop. Peter was seated at the head of one of fifteen tables located in the ballroom with mahogany panels and chandeliers. He sat on red, black, and green satin pillows. He wore the costume page boys wore in the Spanish court. The other brothers and sisters sat before turkey, goose, blackberry pie, and cherry pie, and there were huge bowls of salad on each table and three kinds of wine. And in the middle of it all lay a pig with an apple in its mouth. Black Peter was enjoying his fish and peppers, jerked pork and Dragon's Snout while the others whispered among themselves.

"How dare he remove the face of our Saint from that painting? Why does Boy Bishop always leave that crazy spade behind when he goes on a mission? I've had enough of this painting. Ghetto surrealism, that's what it is." Sister Alice and Sister Barbara were scribbling notes and passing them to each other. One would read a note from the other and giggle.

"If Boy Bishop doesn't return soon, this maniacal and paranoid black is going to take over," said another of Boy Bishop's followers.

"I plan to phone him tonight. If he doesn't get back here soon, there's going to be bloodshed," said Brother James. Sister Barbara pouted and then gave Black Peter a fierce stare. She folded her arms. Her bald head glistened and she wore hooped, gold earrings.

"How come we have to do what you say and accept your painting? Boy Bishop should have the final sayso. I for one don't like what you've done with the painting," she said. The gathering murmured: "You ain't no Rasta anyway. You maybe can fool these white people, but you can't fool me." Sister Alice sat down, triumphantly.

"Bro. Peter is in charge when Boy Bishop leaves. We worked out the details in secret council, and none of you is to question that." Everybody ceased their whispering. Brother Andrew had been with Boy Bishop longer than anybody. He'd gone to school with him and had been a guest at the mansion owned by Bishop's father, Herman Schneider, the late department store president. "Peter, perhaps the anxiety of the group would be allayed if you'd just explain some of the symbolism in that painting. I rather like it." Sisters Barbara and Alice glared at Brother Andrew.

"His name ain't no Peter," said Sister Barbara, one of the whores who'd defected from Joe Baby. "He's a crazy nigger that Boy Bishop dragged up from Forty-second Street."

"Give him a chance," Andrew said.

"I can tell you why I put the face of Haile Selassie in the place of Saint Nicholas. Because they are both one and the same," said Peter.

"One and the same?" Andrew said. "I don't follow you."

"Look at it this way," Peter said, climbing down from his seat and walking towards the painting. He climbed atop a chair and began pointing to his work of art.

"Now, see, here is the Emperor who rode on a white horse the same as Nicholas and the same as Marcus Garvey, who predicted that the Emperor was coming."

"Who was Marcus Garvey?" someone asked.

"An Obeah man from Jamaica. He was the prophet who was sent by Jah to pave the way for the coming of the Emperor.

"Now, let me explain to you," said Black Peter, whose whale's head contrasted with his small body. "There," he pointed out, "you see the Emperor punish the teef just the way Nicholas did. The Emperor punish the teef Mussolini." He pointed to Mussolini's head in the painting. Mussolini had the body of a dog. Black Peter's painting showed the Emperor bringing down a machete on the Italian dictator's head.

"Nicholas fly, the ashanti fly, and here you see Selassie flying to the League of Nations where he went to protest the invasion of Ethiopia by Rome. The Emperor had his problems with Rome. As you know, the Vatican removed Nicholas from the calendar of Saints." Some of the nuns who were loyal to Peter looked on as Peter ran down his "science," as he called it. His "reasoning." "Nicholas is an island patron. The patron of New York Island. The Emperor is also an island patron. The Island of Jamaica."

"Isn't he adorable?" said one nun.

"He's wonderful," said another. "If you look closely, you'll see that he's wearing an aura."

"Selassie was the Emperor of Ethiopia, Ethiopia is Zion. Nicholas was once overseer of a monastery named New Zion," Black Peter argued.

Another nun who was loyal to Boy Bishop, named Sister Suggs, glared heat at the nuns who were admiring Peter as he continued his, for Sister Suggs, "wild, incoherent, and 'scattershot' narrative." She mangled her french bread and held her mouth open as she stared at Peter. When Peter finished, a hush filled the room.

"I have to hand it to you, Brother Peter. You are an excellent painter [Sister Barbara passed a note to Sister Alice and they both grinned at each other] and I agree that we must keep up with the times. I think, however, that we should wait for the return of the Boy Bishop. Tell me more about this Rastafarianism. It sounds fascinating."

"Thank you, Brother Andrew." Suddenly, Brother Peter hesitated. He moved his neck about as though it were the hood of a black cobra.

"Where's Brother James and that journalist woman?"

11

Washington streets were heavy with icy mush. Winter, again, was behaving peculiarly. Some blamed it on the ozone belt, and others said man-made chemicals. The President was seated in the Oval Office. There was a knock at the door and then the knob turned. It was his wife. She was carrying a tiny box covered with glossy black wrapping paper.

"Mummy," he said, "what's that you have in your hand?"

She gave him the package. "Well, what do we have here," he said, opening it. "Jade cuff links. Thanks, dear, but Christmas hasn't even arrived."

"My dearest darling," she said, "every day has been Christmas since we've been together. My beautiful husband. Every woman says so. Your face on the cover of all the magazines. Women staring at you across the state dinner tables. Even the queen, when she was introduced to you. Her voice became husky; she had to clear her throat."

"Yes, those state dinners. I adore the French food, but I don't know. Sometimes I get the feeling that people are laughing at me behind my back."

"I know things have been hard, dear, but Bob takes care of all of the serious decisions. I mean war and peace and worrisome things like that, and all we have to do is throw parties and ride horses. It's such a sweet life, dear, and the people love you."

"They love Santa Claus more."

"O, but he comes only once a year."

"Yeah, but each season he seems to come earlier and leave later. One of these days he's going to get heavy in the head from all the publicity they've given him, and hang around until after the twenty-fifth. The season has gotten longer since 1981 when it ended on January twentieth, Inaugural Day."

His wife walked over to him and sat on his lap. She was still in good shape. Very good shape. She was a dark, alluring woman who had a merry laugh, but she could be a terror.

"Dear, I've been thinking. You know I am the President of the United States and they ought to at least tell me what's going on from time to time. I mean, I've been watching television a lot and I feel that some of these problems—"

"Don't worry your handsome autumn-leaf red hair about any of this. Those vulgar practical men can deal with the problems of . . . of society and things. You just sit here in the Oval Office, splendid as a Dior butterfly, smile at the little Four-H Club delegations, kiss the March of Dimes poster child. They all adore you."

"How's the White House restoration coming?"

"The White House is in a mess. Yesterday, the ceiling collapsed in the press room. Luckily, no conference was being held that day. Some of the newsmen would have been injured. The electricity system has to be repaired too. The fire department says it's a hazard."

He took hold of her long, smooth arm just above a diamond bracelet.

"Thanks for having faith in me, Elizabeth. But I'm scared. It looks so different from the inside. I'm beginning to question my beliefs. It's not like campaigning. Campaigning was so much fun. Meeting all those people. The balloons streaming down. But now it seems that everything I've built up, everything I've worked for is just one big joke, one huge laughable joke, and I'm beginning to have doubts about those

things I learned in school, sometimes I think, then I think: not
Pat O'Brien and Gregory Peck. They couldn't have been
lying." He put his head into his hands and began to sob. "All
I've worked for a joke, one big laughable joke." He got the
sniffles. The President's eyes became misty.

"Dear, you shouldn't say that. Don't ever say that. The
people. The small people. The little people all over America
see you as their friend. You've created a nation they can all
respect. Nobody spits on the United States any more. With you
in office, the nation is walking proud. You can see the people.
Walking proud."

"How did I get mixed up in this? There I was in Congress,
doing all right. I didn't have any ambition above that. I took the
vice-presidency because nobody else wanted it. How did I know
that the President would die in office? Granted, he was ninety-
one years old when they elected him, but he was in good
shape. Passing all of his physicals, and then, flop, he was gone,
just like that. And then the Secretary of Defense, committing
suicide. The scandals. And now this . . . this new problem.
Just think, only ten years ago they were the buffoons of the
world. Remember how much we used to make fun of what's
his name? You know, the one whose mother would eat a
cannibal? And now look at that country. High megatech bucks.
Threatening us. Incidents at sea over fishing rights. We can't
get the Soviet Union to help us. They're bogged down in the
Baltic States, chasing sheepherders through the mountains.
The Latvians have entered their third week sitting-in at the
University, and some of the Russian troops are weeping at the
beauty of their folk songs. Moscow is flustered and can't pay
back its loan to Chase Manhattan. But enough of that. How is
Anne? Is Anne coming home for Christmas? Is she still mad at
us?"

"She's still in the sanitorium, dear. She has so many drugs
in her she can hardly stand up. But it's for her own good. She's
such a throwback to the sixties, her idealism. She still can't

understand why you permitted the chairman of the American Nazi Party to meet with you in the White House. I told her you could never have carried Conta Costra County in California without his help. She just didn't understand that we had to carry California. So young and so vulnerable. She was always embarrassing us. Demonstrating for this or that cause. Raising funds for the South Carolina refugees. Those people shouldn't have been living in South Carolina in the first place. She was always bringing in stray causes from the cold. It is happening to the children of all our friends. Look, look at them. The suicides, the drunkenness; it's just something in the air."

"But, dear, this is getting bad. Why, one of the Secret Service men said that Washington is full of starving people, that some of them are dying in the streets, sick with sores all over them. They're living in tent cities they built in the parks. That if it weren't so cold it would look like some starving famished country, the only difference being that the flies hate the cold. Thousands of people are dropping dead in the snow. I read about it in the newspapers, I think. O, I wish my son were here. He was so smart. He used to read things to me.

"There's still no news from the F.B.I. about who's responsible for the death of our son. Mummy, I have a good idea. Why don't we go visit our farm in the Catskills. This place gives me the creeps sometimes. Why, I read somewhere that this place is haunted. That people have seen the ghosts of George Washington, Dwight Eisenhower, Andrew Jackson, and Harry Truman walking through the halls, crying, and wailing. They're heroes. Why would they be doing that?"

"Now, Dean, you know what happened the last time you took that three-month vacation. There was an outcry from the public. They want you to be visible. They'll start gossiping— you know, your reputation."

"What reputation, Mummy?"

"Well, dear, the public doesn't think you're very bright."

"I may not be an intellectual giant, Mummy, but I'm as smart as the next fellow. That White House aide, Bob Krantz—he was my friend during the campaign. But now I haven't seen him since the inaugural. If he'd give me more responsibility, I'd show that I know a thing or two. He never asks my advice about a damned thing, and do you know what? I'm getting pretty sore. Why, I look like a fool in front of the press. I don't know what's going on and it's supposed to be my government." Mrs. Clift moved behind the desk and comforted her husband.

"Mummy," the President said.

"Yes, hon."

"When are we going to take a ride on the Presidential yacht again? That was fun. All those Congressmen coming up and shaking my hand. They knew all the ball scores."

"Yes, but their wives. They almost toppled you into the Potomac, they were grabbing on you so." Dean held Elizabeth's hand. "I have an idea," she said. "Why don't we do what we used to do during the campaign?"

"What's that, dear?"

"I'll bring up a couple of bottles of Dom Perignon and some corned beef sandwiches and we'll have a late snack and watch the late show."

"O, that sounds like fun, Mummy. I'll enjoy that. But where are you going now?"

"I have to light the White House Christmas tree. They just delivered it from Alaska and all of the decorations are up."

Rev. Jones sat, his stern black eyes hidden by the dark glasses he always wore. Across from the Reverend sat Robert Loss, chairman of Rahab Petroleum. General Lionel Matthews sat at another end of the long black walnut conference table, his subzero eyes unblinking, seemingly in a fog, thinking, no doubt, of the millions he'd sent to the land of ghosts. Robert Reynolds, the Beer King and organizer of the money that brought the ex-model, President Dean Clift, to office, sat looking over some notes. He was brittle and edgy. He almost missed the meeting. Some Indians were giving his company problems. They claimed that the water which went into Regal Beer came from one of their sacred springs. There were also representatives from Japan, Germany, and South Africa in attendance.

Some of the men were glum because the Rev. Jones had used the benediction as an opportunity to deliver a stinging rebuke to the West, mentioning the pitfalls that lay ahead if it continued fornicating, drinking, pot-smoking, and all around Frenching about. The men had applauded him. They all wore the same striped ties, black shoes, and dark suits. Rev. was now nursing a tall expensive scotch provided by one of the formal, tuxedoed waiters. The others were fidgeting with their fifty-dollar ballpoint pens, or had their heads buried in the *Wall Street Journal*, *Barron's*, *U. S. News and World Report*, and *Human Events*. They had finished some of the items on their agenda and were waiting for Bob Krantz, Rev. Jones's protege, to deliver a report on his ingenious plan to solve a major domestic and foreign problem. Jones was proud of Bob Krantz. It was the Reverend, one of the principal investors in President Dean Clift, who had brought Bob Krantz, a former television executive, into the government. At first they had been opponents.

There had been a confrontation between Krantz, the Whyte B.C.'s lawyers, and Rev. Jones and some of the higher-ups of his television ministry, whose mission was to purify the TV Babylon. What worked in Texas didn't work in New York. Rev. Jones had easily intimidated the local television stations in the Lone Star State, the result being that the stations refused to carry programs the Reverend condemned for their licentious-ness and obscenity.

Emboldened by this success, Reverend and his men had called for a boycott of Whyte B.C., only to have Bob Krantz reveal certain aspects of the Reverend's career the Reverend didn't want brought up. The Reverend had called off the boycott, but God Moves in Mysterious Ways, it is said. Turns out that while Rev. Jones and his people were on the way to a huge Jesus rally in Los Angeles, they came upon the scene of a fiery accident. The rich Italian sports car had overturned several times and the victim, pinned underneath, was crying for help. The Reverend had gone to Krantz's aid and, without thinking, had lifted the car while others removed Krantz. It was nothing short of a miracle.

Cocaine, the Inca's revenge upon the Europeans, had told Krantz to drive off a cliff on the way to his Malibu hideaway. This phantom drug, which moves like cotton, had almost devoured Krantz. After his recuperation in the hospital, Krantz had joined Rev. Jones and gone to work as his promotions man. Thousands of new souls had gone over to Christ as a result of Krantz's knowledge of direct mail and television.

Dressed in a conservative plaid-gray suit, Krantz strode into the room. Admiral Matthews, Rev. Jones, and Robert Reynolds smiled. He nodded towards the men and greeted the delegates. A woman who had followed Krantz into the room began passing out mints to the delegates, from a basket.

"Gentlemen, we've flown you in from capitals of the world because we've found a method by which we may eliminate both the surplus people who, by sheer numbers, are taking over our country, and the foreign menace as well. We've found it necessary to take drastic action to end this, this problem once and for all. You know how foolish we were from the end of the Second World War to the 1980s, when we thought that the Soviet Union was the main problem. Since the early eighties, they've been bound down in endless land wars in Asia, plus uprisings in the satellite countries, and now this Riga thing."

"Reggae?" grumped the delegate from the United Kingdom. "We've banned that seditious music in my country. We've gotten nothing but trouble from those people."

"No, not Reggae, Riga. The ancient capital of Latvia. It started a celebration of independence, which came to the country on November 18, 1918, and then as these things go, the blasted thing got out of hand. Some terrorists began ringing bells at St. Peter's church—a church the Russians burned once. O, I don't have to tell you how these feuds become so deep and confusing, and then someone toppled the statue of Lenin, the Russian troops fired into the crowd, and now they have their hands full and the damned thing has spread into Estonia and Lithuania; and with the unrest among the Muslim population and resounding defeats in Africa and South America, gentlemen, I'm afraid that the Soviet empire is melting like butter. But what really brought the free world and our Russian allies together, as you know, was the South Carolina incident.

"In 1987, we signed that peace treaty with the Soviet Union because we felt that if a nuclear conflagration happened between us, all that would remain would be the Southern Hemisphere and the world would turn brown and muddy and resound with bongo drums, half-clad people lying on the beach, carnivals, rum, gambling, Aloha shirts, mangoes, and the mad savage drumming and the strumming of guitars and everyone would live in grass huts and the world would just go to pot.

"Those were years of unlimited optimism. We didn't really need those miserable slave pits around the world any more, thus taking the steam out of many a revolutionary's anger, and so we built space ships which began to travel throughout the solar system mining for resources, and when the robot passengers wore out, they reproduced themselves, and the vital people became enormously wealthy, and for them every day became Christmas, but we forgot one thing. All of those surplus people, reproducing like mink. We tried spermacide, and sterilization, but it didn't work. We contemplated germ warfare but ruled that out because some of the surplus people were mixed up with the vital people. And then the surplus nations got ahold of the bombs." A man entered the room, holding a telephone which rested on a pillow. "O, what is it?" Bob Krantz said, scornfully.

"It's your wife."

"O, very well." He picked up the phone. "Excuse me, gentlemen. What on earth is it?" he said. "O, I'm sorry. Yes, I know, it's been three months since I've been home. O, I'm sorry to hear that. When is the funeral? Don't be absurd. You know I can't get away; I'll have the secretary send some flowers. Yes, now I have to go. Goodbye." The man apologized to the gathering.

"I'm sorry, gentlemen, you know how these minor domestic matters sometimes intrude upon the business at hand. Seems my son was killed in a car accident.

"Now, as I was saying, surplus people began to take over our cities and we found that we could perform technological miracles but we couldn't get rid of the surplus people, and we couldn't get rid of the bombs which lay in depots all over the country, fermenting like dragons' eggs, leaking. We were very lucky that no one stumbled or breathed too hard in those places, and then the clumsy bastard working in a South Carolina depot sneezed and dropped one while loading a truck.

"The very next year Nigeria exploded one and then Uganda." The delegates murmured.

"Yes, Uganda. We couldn't have expected that these nations would spend an eternity under military rule and under unemployed intellectuals. A generation got down to business and now not only do they have bombs but they have the delivery systems so precise that they could lob one right into this conference room from one of their capitals." The delegates looked over their shoulders. One rose, and went to the window.

"Early in the eighties, the surplus people were multiplying at such an alarming rate that they were beginning to gain on the vital population. It was then decided to create an artificial famine and we elected, O, what's his name? O, you know the one with the wife who changed her clothes eight times a day and was always hallucinating about ghosts in the White House bathtubs, and you remember he began hanging out at the Irish Club in Washington, and before you knew it he was on the radio making speeches for the I.R.A., and then went crazy altogether and changed his name to O'something. The damn fool divorced his wife, disowned his horsey daughter and his epicene son, and returned to some dreadful place called the village of Ballyporeen in the County Tipperary."

"Yes, I know the place well, perfectly awful place, people with dirty faces and no flowers in their homes," said the delegate from the United Kingdom.

"And now he hangs out in a pub telling stories and commuting to Dublin where he's working on his memoirs. The artificial famine was supposed to deprive the surplus people of energy and rehabilitative service by eliminating free lunches, food stamps, and medical care, but they kept on keeping on, as one of their illiterate spokesmen once said. The surplus people took over our cities—not only in the East, but San Francisco in the West, Albuquerque, San Antonio in the Southwest, Miami in the South. The vital people ran out of suburbs and high-rise buildings to flee, and so we built bubble cities at the bottom of the sea and sent them there, and you know what happened. They went crazy, staring at exotic fish all day. And so we sent them to populate space stations, and nobody wanted them out there. We thought we had someone in President Orrin Roberts, and you all know what happened. He got himself caught committing sodomy and smoking hashish in a Washington park. We tried desperately to get him off, but because he was caught underneath one of our monuments, a sculpture of the flag-raising at Iwo Jima, the public demanded his hide." The Japanese delegates folded their arms, stared at their watches nervously, and gave one another the once-over.

"And now we have the first male model in office and things can't be better. We're finally able to do away with the surplus people once and for all. He's a real dummy whose IQ is about fifty-five." The men laughed. "But he has some kind of animal appeal. The women, even men, can't keep their hands off him. He won't shy away from the script the way the actor did, and he's such an active heterosexual he won't embarass us behind public statues. He's just content fidgeting with his lapels and dabbing hair cream into his palms. He spends hours in front of the mirrors. He removed all of the portraits from the Blue Room and replaced them with ones of himself from different ad campaigns." The delegates roared with laughter.

There was a commotion at the end of the table. Krantz called for order. "What's wrong?" he asked. The head of the South African government-in-exile raised his hand and was recognized by the speaker. His "government" had fled South Africa taking billions of dollars' worth of gold and had taken up residence on a small island off South Africa. From this island they were launching guerilla attacks against the mainland and were building a nuclear arsenal with which to menace the nations of Africa.

"It's the West German delegate, Mr. Krantz," the South African delegate said. "He's sitting here crying and trembling like a dryer. His face is ashen, and he's—he's—"

"I can speak, I can speak for myself," the West German delegate said. "Just help me to my feet." Other delegates helped him. He wiped his eyes.

"Fellow delegates," he began. "I apologize if I don't seem to be myself, but I couldn't help reflecting upon the irony of your words, Mr. Krantz, and the dilemma you find yourself in.

My grandfather was with the Führer and we grew up on stories about our great leader's last days in the bunker, and how he paced around the room, his uniform disheveled, right there showing you something was wrong because the Leader was so immaculate—and his breath was dirty and his eyes wet and bloodshot and in a fixed gaze, and how he went on and on about how he was the prophet of the white race's destiny and how you all ridiculed him."

"We didn't," said the representative of the South African government-in-exile.

"Not you, my friend, but many of you did," the West German said to the delegates, now many of them sobbing or with their heads lowered, "and you ridiculed him and made fun of his height and called his government some kind of vaudeville act. He spoke of how you despised him. O, it hurt him so, and then you pounded the living daylights out of him, and he was only concerned about you and your future. He warned you about the negrification of Europe and the Jewing of America. And now you're faced with the mongrelization of the world, and it's your fault. It's your fault—what you did to that man. You fools, for you to have dishonored this man so. You called him a monster and a devil, but now you need him; you need him to guide you before the Southern Hemisphere creeps over the planet. You wouldn't listen to him. You persecuted him. This prophet. This great man." He sat down. There was a long silence. Finally, the delegate from the U.S. spoke up.

"May I inform the West German delegate that Congress has set aside an American holiday to celebrate the Führer's birthdate and not only that, our President met with the chairman of the American Nazi Party, who appeared in storm-trooper's uniform and left by the front door of the White House. We gave him a twenty-one gun salute and their meeting was said to have been a warm exchange of views."

Krantz finally called for order. "Although I sympathize with the West German delegate's feelings, we must keep the meeting going or we'll never finish. And now, gentlemen, we'd like to spend the next hour discussing Operation Two Birds."

There was a lock down, similar to the ones they have in jails. Boy Bishop had ordered everybody to their rooms. Bishop and Brother Peter were having it out. The only other Nicolaites present were Brother James and Brother Andrew. There was no expression on Black Peter's whale-like face as Boy Bishop berated him with a barrage of criticisms, and though the gathering knew Black Peter's ventriloquial abilities, they were still startled but pretended not to show it when Black Peter would respond to the Boy Bishop's charges in Boy Bishop's voice, using the exact tone and inflections Boy Bishop used.

"I want that painting back up, and that's my decision," Boy Bishop said, casting a cold and sneering blue eye upon the oil painting that still hung. Brother James smiled. To think that this wretched little toad—when Black Peter wasn't looking like a whale, he resembled a toad—had deprived him of a little publicity by demanding that he and the journalist Jamaica Queens return from the garden to the feast.

"Aren't you being inflexible, Boy Bishop?" Black Peter answered, coolly, calmly. "Don't you see that both Nicholas and Selassie were Rasta? Think of how both had to die before they could accomplish something beneficial for mankind— how both had insignificant careers until they were reborn as symbols, or miracle workers."

"Haile Selassie was a tyrant," Bishop said.

"The historical career of legends is unimportant," Peter said, a glowing smile now sweeping his face. The smile nudged Brother James. He didn't know which one he envied more, Peter or Boy Bishop.

"Why are you even listening to this con man, Boy Bishop? You can see he's crazy. If this plan to substitute this Ethiopian charlatan for Saint Nicholas is insane, the other one, his body-snatching plan, is as loony as they come," Brother James offered.

"Yes, he's reckless. But some of the followers have begun to listen to him, and if we don't give him a fair hearing they'll criticize us. Nicholas was a just Saint. Remember how he intervened on the side of the three generals when they were to be unjustly executed by Emperor Constantine?" Brother James frowned.

"I'm glad you brought that up," Brother Andrew said. "Some of us don't believe that Brother Peter should even be going through this ordeal." Brother James and Boy Bishop were stunned.

"Seems to me that Black Peter is merely trying to bring us into modern times. How many of the young can relate to Saint Nicholas, a senile Saint? If you think that Santa Claus is a vulgar creation from the demonic pen of Thomas Nast, then you can at least accept Selassie. He's legend. That's why this Reggae thing is big. It should bring us some followers."

"I'm not on trial here; Peter is," Boy Bishop said.

"I wouldn't be too sure about that," Brother Andrew said.

"He's gotten to you! You're talking just like him, and your hair—what the fuck are you doing to your hair!" demanded Brother James.

"I'm not taking any sides," Brother Andrew said. "Some of us simply believe that Boy Bishop has strayed away from our little community. He seems to enjoy hobnobbing with the rich. See how he appears with them so much in the newspapers.

Charity balls, tennis matches, endless parties on estates of more than one hundred acres!"

"I think they call it fund-raising," Boy Bishop said. "How do you think this place exists from month to month? The collections in the streets and airports don't even pay the heating bill."

"There are other ways," Peter said. "If we'd follow my plan, we wouldn't have to worry about money. We'd have power which is worth more than money. I agree with Brother Andrew," Peter said. "You've spent too much time away from us. You're out of touch. I say that we end all this currying favor of the rich and adopt my plan."

"Your wild scheme will bring about the downfall of this organization. It's a crazy vision intruding upon reality. All of this nonsense about your being able to send dreams and visions to the President. And your body-snatching plan. It won't work," Boy Bishop snarled.

"It will work," Peter said. "We need to do something daring to impress the young if we want followers. With my extraordinary ventriloquial abilities, we can do it. And Tarpon Springs—"

"Why are we listening to this crazy spade?" Brother James said. "Everybody knows that's nothing but some silly mysticism. The product of peasant superstitions like the one about a Nicholas ikon that bled. What nonsense," Brother James said.

"I agree," said Boy Bishop, weakly.

"You agree!" Black Peter said. "So you believe with Brother James that these miracles didn't really happen."

"Your lapse of faith is really a serious matter, Boy Bishop," Brother Andrew said. Black Peter smiled. His mocking smile angered Boy Bishop.

"Look, you filthy little gnat, if it weren't for me you'd be down on Forty-second Street asking passersby to distinguish between you and that shabby little dummy you used to have." Black Peter scowled. Brother James chuckled.

"That one always gets the sooty son-of-a-bitch."

"That does it," said Brother Andrew. "Racism has no place in our community. You will recall that Saint Nicholas himself was Turkish. If you cannot accept Brother Peter, then you would not accept Saint Nicholas. And this convinces me more than ever that we should adopt Selassie to substitute for Nicholas. We need the Ethiopian as a gesture to the third world that we're not just a bunch of white boys performing a fraternity prank. That we're serious."

"I think Brother Andrew has put the whole question as eloquently as anybody could. Thank you, Brother Andrew."

"Thank *you*, Brother Peter," Andrew said.

"Andrew, what's come over you," Boy Bishop pleaded. "Don't you see, he's trying to divide us with his harebrained schemes. He's not after the oil companies which control Christmas. He's after something else. I've had enough of this reasoning, as you call it. I have the right to take that painting from the wall and I will order it removed at once. I built this organization with my bare hands. I was the brains behind it, and I'm not going to have it undermined by some vagrant from Forty-second Street. What a fool I was to permit you to stay here until you found another dummy. A gesture of kindness."

"Aw, don't be such a wimp, Boy Bishop," Andrew said. "Peter has breathed new life into this place. He's an elemental force, like Poseidon, rising from beneath the waters— Poseidon, Nicholas's ancestor. There hasn't been this much energy in this place in a long time."

"I want the painting down!" Boy Bishop screamed, and his scream could be heard in the rooms in the upper part of the house where the followers remained, locked in, waiting for the outcome of the debate—the showdown that had been coming for a long time—waiting to be summoned.

"It's not going to be that simple, Boy Bishop. I suggest that we call a meeting and have the entire assembly take part in this decision. We can also discuss your position in this society."

"Boy Bishop runs this organization," Brother James said. "What he says goes."

"But we have our rights, too," Black Peter said.

"What about your treatment of that journalist, Jamaica Queens? Ordering her out. Your rudeness to James," Bishop asked.

"She was an interloper. No better than those two troublesome whores you brought in from the street, Sister Alice and Sister Barbara," Black Peter said. "They have no respect for me." Just then, Boy Bishop's secretary interrupted the meeting and whispered to Boy Bishop. Boy Bishop excused himself. They heard a shot, followed by Boy Bishop's screams, and rushed from the room.

14

It happened in 1985. The court reporters, bailiffs, guards, news vendors could tell their grandchildren about it. All of these men, scores of them, dressed in red suits, big black belts, typing-paper-white beards, blue eyes, ruddy cheeks, conferring with their lawyers. Some who tingled little bells were told by Judge Swallow to cut it out. His face was flushed. The hearing was held after lunch. Oswald Zumwalt's lawyers were there, too. There were Salvation Army Santa Clauses, department store Santa Clauses, Santa Clauses from the V.A. and children's hospitals. There were Christmas pageant Santa Clauses, and charity Santa Clauses, and Santa Clauses who entertained the very rich. There were black, red, and white Santa Clauses.

Judge Swallow dismissed the class action suit and it stood that Oswald Zumwalt owned the exclusive right to Santa Claus, as well as his aliases, Kris Kringle and Saint Nick, and even old Nick. All of the department stores, candy manufacturers, toy executives, and other components of a billion-dollar industry would have to deal with him.

Zumwalt was now getting a bill through Congress which would give him twenty thousand acres of land at the North Pole for his Christmas Land, to which consumers from all over the world would fly, Supersaver, to celebrate Christmas. A multibillion-dollar city under a dome as well as a space station where future Zumwalt Clauses would fly to earth.

What became known as the Santa Claus decision was based upon the Lone Ranger decision, which prevented the original Lone Ranger, Clayton Moore, from wearing the Lone Ranger mask he'd worn for many years. This remarkable California decision was handed down about eight months before another California decision which outlawed the naturalistic novel.

About a year after the Lone Ranger decision, Clayton Moore, now wearing what the newspapers referred to as his "ubiquitous dark glasses," attended the funeral of Jay Silverheels. The company that won the Lone Ranger trademark couldn't wait until Jay Silverheels was cold in his grave before they began casting about for a new Lone Ranger and Tonto. This Tonto had trouble saying kemo sabe.

The aging thespian whom Zumwalt hired to play Santa Claus became so popular with the children that their wrath at the Zumwalt decision—eggnog trucks were overturned, geese were cooked—turned to love for the new Santa Claus. After hype and p.r., they would have no other Santa Claus but Zumwalt's Claus.

Zumwalt began the season on the last Saturday in

November. Saint Nicholas is the Big Apple's patron saint; a town of give and take, of people dishing it out and people on the receiving end. On that day, the Zumwalt party would move into Manhattan from a hidden estate on Staten Island called "Spain" because of its hacienda style. The next day they would mount a barge and float across the river to Manhattan Island, accompanied by water-spouting tugboats.

Zumwalt stood in one of Spain's lavish conference rooms. "And over here," Zumwalt said, pointing to the map, "we plan to build forty-eight restaurants, eighteen bars, and there will be a village of Bethlehem which will stretch to about eight hundred acres. We'll have the Church of the Nativity over there. We'll charge five bucks to get into that; in the rear of the church, we'll build a coffee shop and souvenir shop. Everybody'll want to see that. And up here, Congressman, will go the North Star. With the computer we have to run Christmas Land, we'll be able to brighten it or dim it whenever we wish." Zumwalt was in pinstripes and black shoes. The Congressman's rattlesnake-skin cowboy boots were stretched across the coffee table which held the map. His stetson was on the floor.

"This is one great project, Mr. Zumwalt. I got to hand it to you. You pulled it off. Now I have some concrete proposals to make to the committee. One thing, though."

"What's that, Congressman Kroske?"

"Well. We got some beechnuts on the committee who seem to be getting a lot of Jew money from the Northeast. They're worried about what's going to happen to the wildlife up there. What shall I tell 'em?"

"They're worried about the ice. America has become the colony of the world, and they're worried about the fucking ice. You tell those fuckers that we'll keep their precious little ecosystem intact. We won't harm a single penguin. It's the Eskimos who are getting in our way."

"That ought to please them. And, Mr. Zumwalt, thanks for inviting me over here. They're all waiting for you tomorrow. Why, Bowling Green Park is packed. Some are carrying their sleeping bags and have been waiting for several days. Everybody's waiting for tomorrow. The schools are closed. There are lights up and down Fifth Avenue. Carol-singing in Central Park.

"There are traffic jams in the snow. People are pouring into New York from all over the country for the festivities. The hotels are full. You can't get a reservation."

"We'll give them a show, Congressman. Why don't you come over for the cocktail reception at Gracie Mansion. I'm sure the Mayor would like to see you. He's going to black-up and entertain the private dinner with his imitation of Al Jolson."

"Sorry, Mr. Zumwalt, but I think I'll be heading back to Washington. The situation isn't so hot in our nation's capital these days."

"I've been following the papers. What's the latest?"

"I saw the President last week. He was signing a bill that Adolf Hitler be given posthumous American citizenship. He looked pretty bad. You wouldn't believe he was the most famous model of the eighties, his face adorning thousands of billboards. I hear he's soaking up bourbon like it was water. The skin on his face hangs like a bloodhound's. His eyes look like two Japanese flags. Things look bad. The economy looks real bad. A loaf of bread costs fifty dollars."

"We have a great Christmas campaign this year. It ought to give the U.S. a full stocking. We expect billions in sales."

"That sure will help things, Mr. Zumwalt. I'll try to get down to the annual Christmas Eve celebration at Madison Square Garden."

"I'll leave a couple of tickets for you and the missus, Congressman."

"Thanks, Zumwalt. I'd appreciate that." The Congressman rose and shook hands with Zumwalt, now on his feet. Jack Frost picked up Zumwalt's stetson and handed it to him. They headed towards the door. The Congressman turned to Santa Claus.

"And thank you, Santa, for signing those autographs for the kids. You'll soon be in your new home at the North Pole if everything works out. The kids talk about you all the time. You really are a moral force, because it's at Christmas when people bury the hatchet and spread good cheer." Santa smiled.

"And don't worry about the bill," the Congressman said, turning to Zumwalt. "Once it's out of committee, it's as good as through. I don't expect a fight in the House or the Senate. The North Pole Development Corporation has friends in both houses. You can count on your friends, Mr. Zumwalt," the Congressman said, winking. Jack Frost: black suit, shirt, sequined tie, shiny wet black hair pinned to scalp, bad eye, helped the Congressman into his deerskin jacket.

"By the way, Congressman," Zumwalt said, "Merry Christmas." He handed the Congressman a gift-wrapped box. The Congressman's eyes widened.

"Thank you, Mr. Zumwalt. Thank you." The Congressman left. Arms folded, Jack Frost leaned against the wall. Zumwalt turned to S.C.

"You did it again," Zumwalt said.

Santa Claus was puzzled.

"O, don't play coy with me. I heard about it. At the Macy's reception downstairs. You were seen talking to a young lady. A buyer. You've forgotten that the contract requires you only to say Ho-Ho-Ho. And what would you like to have for Christmas, little boy, or little girl, or little person."

"I'm sorry, Mr. Zumwalt. It won't happen again."

"I'm sorry, he says. You have a good job here. If it weren't for this job you'd be in a nursing home, glued to the Betamax. Watching your lousy soap opera reruns. Rex Stuart. Wasn't that your name before you got this job? The North Pole Development Corporation gave you new life. The North Pole Development Corporation rescued Christmas. Made it

what it is today. Both you and the season would be out of a job
if it weren't for my genius."

"I'm very aware of that, Mr. Zumwalt," Santa said.

"OK. You can go. Get a good night's sleep. Tomorrow we
move on to Manhattan. You're going to need your energy."

"Good night, Mr. Zumwalt." Santa rose and started for
the door. Jack Frost sneered at him as he passed him on the
way out. S.C. didn't trust Jack Frost. Jack Frost had been
acquitted of killing his own grandmother, but Santa didn't
believe him. The prosecutor just didn't have enough evidence.
Frost never left any. And if that wasn't bad enough, on the day
of his grandmother's funeral, he went to a musical.

Alone in his room, Santa settled back with a double
bourbon on the rocks. His long white beard stretched to his
belt. Each morning a barber from the North Pole Development, or Big North as the conglomerate was called, trimmed
his beard. He'd been trying to reach Vixen, but the phone was
busy. He wanted to tell her that everything was going as
planned. She was the only one of the brass who would give him
the time of day. He removed his boots and his jacket, and
settled back in the brass bed, taking the newspaper with him.
New York, the City of Saint Nicholas, whose first church was
named for Saint Nicholas, and which boasted a Saint Nicholas
Avenue—whose first Dutch ship wore his face on its stern—
was all geared up for his arrival. The Mayor would be there.
Key officials. They'd be met at the pier. Afterwards, they would
push up to Bowling Green Park. The caravan's pause at
Bowling Green Park was obligatory, for it was on this site that
Oloffe, the Dutchman, had a vision of Saint Nicholas. "And
the sage Oloffe dreamed a dream—and lo, the good St.
Nicholas came riding over the tops of trees, in that self-same
wagon wherein he brings his yearly presents to children, and he
descended hard by where the heroes of Communipaw had
made their late repast. And he lit his pipe by the fire, and sat
himself down and smoked; and as he smoked, the smoke from

his pipe ascended into the air and spread like a cloud overhead."

There was a knock at the door.

15

Saturday went into the kitchen and started to make breakfast. The coffee was ready first. The buzzer rang. He answered the door. He recognized the two men because he'd seen their pictures in the newspaper from time to time. One visitor had been picked up by the police a lot but never convicted. He was standing in the door next to another man, also a folk hero.

"You Nance Saturday?"

"You got him."

"Good, can I come in?" Before Nance could answer, Joe Baby and his companion Big Meat entered the room. Nance Saturday followed them and pointed out some seats.

"Would you like some coffee?"

"Sure," Joe Baby answered, as his companion, Big Meat, nodded his head. Nance brought the coffee into the living room. Joe Baby scanned the room. He rose and went over to the window. He returned to his seat and began another wracking cough.

"So what's on your mind, Joe Baby?"

"They tell me you're good at finding fault."

"Facts. I'm good at discovery."

"Yeah, right, well I need your services." Joe Baby studied Saturday. Joe Baby was wearing a fur hat, coat, and black fur-lined boots. Saturday couldn't glance at Joe Baby's glistening fingers for fear of irritating his eyes.

"Why do you need my services?" Saturday said, glancing at Big Meat and then back at Joe Baby. "There's nothing in this town you can't fix. You know the Mayor."

"Not any more. Those days are gone." Joe Baby began convulsing from a coughing fit.

"What's wrong?" Saturday asked.

"It's his ticker," Big Meat said. "He's having trouble. The doctor says he's in bad shape. He couldn't even make it up the steps just now without my assisting him."

"Look, Nance," Joe Baby finally said. "I'm losing some of my girls. You can't pull the jive on them you used to be able to get away with. They don't want to be number two, you understand. It's a new day. Alice and Barbara took off. I only have two left, and they don't even work half the time. You can't hit them like you used to. You know, twenty years ago they wouldn't give you any trouble, but now they hear all of this agitation from man-haters."

"Man-haters?"

"O, you know," Joe Baby smiled. "They even got women pimping for them nowadays. There's nothing a man can do for them, I mean nothing. Lot of the fellows have gone into legitimate business. Moved to the suburbs. I'm too old to change."

"Why didn't you save your money? When I was a kid I used to see you pushing this thing that looked like a Japanese imperial palace on wheels. Now you're driving that beat-up Seville."

"Beat up is right," Big Meat said. "It's got a quarter of a million miles on it and Joe Baby says it ought to go a quarter of a million miles more."

"When you get rid of it you can sell it to somebody in Saudi Arabia. They like old American cars over there," Saturday said.

"The brothers in Africa have really moved beyond that camel stage. Never thought I'd see the day. Now they're up in space like everybody else. They even have H-Bombs and laser beams and all of the new gadgets they have over here. Charlie thinks twice now before he goes charging into even the smallest countries. Those nuclear weapons are a great equalizer," Joe Baby said.

"Yeah, sure," Nance said. "Look, what do you want me to do?"

"I just want you to get my money back."

"Money?" Nance was confused.

"This kid named Boy Bishop. He took prostitutes off the streets. That was one of his causes. He's giving everybody trouble," Big Meat added.

"Yeah, so much trouble that the boys got together fifty thousand dollars for this Boy Bishop to be blotched," Joe Baby said. "We hired this white boy named Snow Man to do the job because we thought that if one of us did it we'd be spotted and picked up."

"What happened to him?"

"He never came out of their house. Big Meat was going to drive the getaway car, but he waited and waited and Snow Man never showed."

"So what do you fellows want me to do?"

"We want you to find out what happened to Snow Man and my money," Joe Baby said. "Most of all I want you to find out what happened to the fifty thousand."

"I don't know. Cults are dangerous. Ever since Jonestown I've been wary of cults. How much are you going to pay me?"

"Ten thousand."

"Fifteen."

"Fifteen it is."

"I'll find out what happened to Snow Man and, if it's possible, I'll get the money back, if Snow Man is still alive." Joe Baby, Big Meat, and Nance Saturday stood. They shook hands. Joe Baby and Big Meat left.

16

The jukebox was playing "You Keep Me Hanging On." Diana Ross's young, untrained, desperate and heartfelt voice was doing the lead. They were dining in the Boondocks, an ethnic foods restaurant on Tenth Avenue, where catfish was served. One was laid out on Nance's plate. Across from him, his ex, Virginia, sat. She had high cheekbones. Her body didn't have an inch of fat on it, and when she walked the men sighed. She was angry with him, or "upset," as she would say. She was wearing blackberry lipstick which was only a shade darker than her eggplant-colored skin, and she was elegantly educated. Knew about spices and herbs. She traveled a lot, played a lot, and went to brunches. Some of the people in the restaurant were staring at her. She anchored the news sometimes, but she was known mostly for her interview show. Rumor was that she was going to get a top newsman's job after he was fired for "coming on too strong" on the cool medium. He'd complained about the late-movie westerns. He'd work out better on the radio or in the theatre, it was suggested. She was wearing one of those black furs which people like Lauren Bacall and Lillian Hellman model in *The New York Times Magazine* section. She loved that coat. When they were married, he once entered the bedroom, unexpectedly, and found her humping that coat and running her nipples across it. He didn't say nothin. He knew her body like a Laguna knows the weather and, like the Laguna, he knew what that body was capable of doing. But that was a long time ago. And now they were trying to consummate their separation. It had been three years. They just couldn't seem to get around to signing the papers which was frustrating for her because she was always complaining about it. She wanted to be free of him, and he of her. She was always insisting that his hair be cut or that he bathe twice a day, or that he wear a Savile Row suit. It was as though she were a queen bee and he a spider. While the queen bee struggles, the spider waits.

"Are you listening to me?" she asked. He looked up from the catfish, which was just about gone.

"What were you saying?" "You Keep Me Hanging On" was a march.

"I'm asking you why you didn't come to Whyte B.C. last week to sign the papers. Remember you were supposed to?"

"I got hung up on a job."

"A job?"

"Yeah, Joe Baby hired me to get some information for him."

"Joe Baby? You work for somebody like that?"

"What's wrong with Joe Baby?"

"What's wrong with Joe Baby? See, that shows you haven't changed at all. That man makes women go out and peddle themselves for his profit."

"Nobody's twisting their arm. Maybe they like it."

"Incorrigible. If you work for him, you're an accomplice to the continuing crime against women by men."

"Look, I'm not becoming a pimp. I'm doing research for Joe Baby. What's wrong with that?"

"A research assistant, huh? That's what they call people

who beat up people for dictators in foreign countries. That's an appropriate name for you."

"You don't know Joe Baby. He doesn't beat up women. He's civilized. He goes to concerts and things."

"That's a stupid thing to say." The waitress came over and picked up the plates. His is empty. She has left some of the greens and the chitterlings on hers. She hadn't touched the cornbread.

"Would you like some dessert?" the waitress asked.

He ordered some sweet potato pie. She didn't say a thing.

Diana Ross sang of her inability to improve a situation which cast her into a condition of total submissiveness. Another slave of love.

"In the future, I wish you'd be more professional."

"What do you mean?"

"When you can't come on time somewhere, call."

"Yeah, I'm sorry," Nance said. "I know you're busy. Incidentally, I saw that interview you did with Giscard D'Estaing again."

"Where?"

"It was on cable television." He chuckled.

"What's funny?"

"When the interview was over, you embraced him so tightly I thought the man was going to collapse from lack of air."

"You never did like that interview. Good thing you're not a TV reviewer."

"And Mr. Giscard D'Estaing proves once again that the French are the most civilized and humanitarian of the European peoples!"

He was mocking the remarks she made at the conclusion of the interview, D'Estaing seated behind her in his apartment at the Louvre, smiling, thin as a matchstick. Saturday laughed.

"Let's get to the business at hand. I want to be done with this before I go on vacation," she said, frowning.

"Where are you going this year?"

"Jamaica."

"Going down with Mr. Whyte?"

"That's none of your business, Nance. I didn't inquire after those . . . those . . . transient women in your life. That Russian bitch."

She would always bring up "that Russian bitch" referring to an affair he had during their marriage. A friend of hers had spotted them in an Orthodox church eating wafflelike cakes and drinking vodka, as is the custom with Russian people during Lent. Fucking for him and this Russian woman, who had a hyphen in her last name, was fucking for keeps. She was the kind of woman who turned Moussorgsky all the way up so that they had their night on Bald Mountain all right. Other times, they'd make love to Chopin. They'd be tangled up like two bull snakes mating as polonaises trilled and roared around them. And he was keeping up with old Chopin, reaching into the bass clef of her body and plucking at what resided there. He didn't have to fuck her to find pleasure. Just clutching her buttocks and rocking against that healthy Russian landscape was enough, a landscape that swallowed up every invader. He just couldn't keep his hands out of her pants. She did things for him that Virginia refused to do. Virginia was always trying to cover up her country background, but it was the country that made her the beauty she was.

"I can't spend the rest of the evening wrangling with you. My lawyer has marked on the papers the places where you are to sign." She went into her purse. She frantically poked around inside. She'd left the papers at home.

"I'm never going to get out of this," she said. "It's your fault for not coming last week when you said you would."

"Sure, blame me." The waitress brought the check.

"Here, let me," she said. "I can charge this to Whyte B.C."

"I'll pay my half."

"Suit your old stubborn self, Nance."

For the next few days, Nance Saturday watched the comings and goings of the Nicolaites from a Mediterranean restaurant across the street from the mansion. He had gone through a lot of Greek omelettes and salads. Nance was able to identify Sister Alice and Sister Barbara, Joe Baby's former tricks, whom Joe Baby had accused of going over to the white boy, and who were the source of his humiliation in the moribund world of the Pimp. They would spill out of the mansion in the morning, with their begging equipment, and return in the late afternoon. The lights would go out about ten. There was no sign of the Boy Bishop in the group, nor was there any sign of Snow Man.

He spent his mornings in the library gleaning information from old newspaper articles concerning the Nicolaites. There was much information about Boy Bishop. He had graduated at the top of his class, a classics minor, from one of the eastern Ivy League schools; he had stunned friends by entering the priesthood; he was accused by the Vatican of showing too much enthusiasm for the outlaw Saint, Christ's rival, Nicholas. There was a series of articles concerning his excommunication and his reputation among the New England rich as a rogue priest. Boston was a seaport, and since Nicholas was the patron of marine life, the Boy Bishop presided over marine activities. Among the yachtsmen and fishermen he became very adept at raising funds for his organization. After his arrival in New York, he'd received a good deal of notice for his work among the prostitutes in the Times Square area. (Saint Nicholas had rescued three women from prostitution by providing them with a dowry.) One newspaper carried a photo of the society.

Although the newspaper articles were quite interesting, there was nothing in them that would shed light on the disappearance of Snow Man, the cold-blooded assassin hired by Joe Baby. Not a clue. Boy Bishop had certainly disappeared, or was he merely away on a fund-raising trip? And what about Snow Man? Had he disappeared with the money? Had he struck a deal with Boy Bishop? There was nothing about the Nicolaites' routine that would indicate that anything was wrong. Nance Saturday was stuck, but it was usually the other way around: his victims were usually the ones who got stuck. Sooner or later the clues would come to him if his brain kept spinning out feelers. On the third day, his big break came. He had mentioned to Virginia his research on the Nicolaites on Joe Baby's behalf. He was home watching television, "The Kingdom of the Spiders," when the telephone rang. It was Virginia. She knew a fellow journalist named Jamaica Queens who was working on a series of "explosive" articles about the Nicolaites, and yes, she would talk to Saturday.

Saturday entered the lobby on Riverside Drive near 114th Street. On each side of the entrance there was a Chinese vase, dark blue and light blue with some long-beaked, long-legged bird on it. There were black walnut tables and a shiny tiled floor. There was a huge Christmas tree in the Art Deco-style lobby. The elevator had an oval window. The Puerto Rican doorman asked Jamaica Queens was it OK for him to come up; she gave her permission and he rose in the elevator to the seventh floor, where she lived. She was what they'd call a "yellow" woman; she was barefoot and she was wearing a black dress which clung to her body as lovingly as a child would grip its mother's thighs. Her sandy-reddish hair was done up in a frizzy manner, and it had been combed out and nearly reached her waist. She was wearing a bit of rouge on her cat cheeks, and her eyes were the color of nightclub smoke, which was fitting because there was jazz in her walk.

"Mr. Saturday. Please come in." Saturday walked into the apartment and sat on the sofa she directed him to. "Get you a drink?" she asked.

He said he'd like some apple juice if she had it around, and she said that it was no trouble and went into the kitchen. He could see her moving about in the kitchen, opening the door and removing the bottle of apple juice from the refrigerator.

"Was it hard to get a taxi? It's snowing so hard."

"I drove up," he said. When she climbed onto a chair to open a cabinet to fetch him some Fig Newtons, her dress hiked up and he saw a lot of thigh. That yellow skin all of a sudden dominating the black of her dress, decorated with white and red carnations, became too much for him, and his biological imperative almost burst through his trousers. It started to rise like the American flag on Iwo Jima, but Mr. Wigglesworth whispered to him sternly, and so his desire flickered out. Mr. Wigglesworth was his conscience. The old guy kept him out of trouble. There were boxes of unpacked things and he could glance into another room and see that she had begun hanging curtains. He couldn't take his eyes off of her and she began to feel self-conscious, so when she came in from the kitchen with the juice and the Fig Newtons, he pretended to concentrate on the small Christmas tree which stood on a small hall table.

He hadn't paid too much attention to the painting on the wall, but when he saw it, the colors jolted him. I guess that's what it was supposed to do. The title of it was "After Clovis." Naked, midnight-black men with yellow eyes and Playboy-bunny types—naked, supple pink women—were copulating in all manner of positions in a cemetery, by the light of a full moon. Noticing his attention, she mentioned the artist, a well-known black feminist painter. He had seen some of her work all over town, and every time he saw them, the colors jolted him. They were usually about the same subject.

"A striking painting," he said.

"She's done a lot in the same theme," she said.

"I know," he said. "Do you think she'll ever grow?" She gave him a cutting look, then a Hollywood "dahling" smile came across her freckled face.

"She says she's doing her dreams."

"She must have the same dream every night."

"Mr. Saturday, did you want to ask me some questions?" She sat in a chair across from him. She tucked in her legs.

"I'm working for a man who wants me to uncover some information about the Nicolaite Society—Boy Bishop and the rest of them. My ex-wife, Virginia Saturday, said you could help me. I was reading articles in the newspapers about the group. I've been watching the mansion, and I can't find what I'm looking for. If you help me, I would certainly appreciate it." She rose and walked over to the other side of the room, revealing a glide that had a tinge of model-runway walk. There was quite a bit of aplomb in that glide. She returned to her seat.

"I hate a lot of glaring light. It's hard on the eyes. I need my eyes for my work. Mr. Saturday, I did spend some time interviewing some members of the Nicolaites, but I don't know everything there is to know about them. They're quite hermetic. It's hard to get close to them." He showed her a photo of Snow Man that Joe Baby had given to him.

"Did you ever see this man there? Snow Man?"

"No. I don't remember anyone vaguely resembling him. They were all pretty thin, anorexic if you ask me. So, you're Virginia's ex? How long did you two last together?"

"One year."

"What happened?"

"It's a long story. She, well, she thought that I was a slob. She was always trying to get me to comb my hair, or bathe three times a day, or wear a tie. She was fanatical about me combing my hair. She said that when she was a child, her stepfather once tried to strangle her with his hair."

"I think I can help you. I like you. Virginia didn't tell me much about you except—"

"Virginia's a country girl, and she has a country girl's paranoia. Regardless of the original Paris fashions she wears, and the eyelashes, she'd like nothing better than to fling off those fancy shoes and run in the mud."

"She doesn't take any jive from those people at work. I wish I could be like her. Tough. Right now she's in competition with Ms. Ming, that Chinese-American woman. I hear they had a hair-pulling fight in the ladies' room. Mr. Whyte has to decide which one's going to take Bob Riverside's job." Riverside was a Native-American anchor man who was in trouble with Whyte B.C. for complaining about the cowboy-Indian reruns that were broadcast on the network. Mr. Whyte had requested an apology from Riverside, but Riverside refused. Gossip in the industry had it that Riverside would soon be out of a job.

"Virginia's not so tough. You forget, I lived with her for a year. That was some year. But listen, tell me more about the Nicolaites. What did you uncover?"

"I never ran across a Snow Man or nobody in the group mentioned him to me. What did you want him for?"

"He owes my client some money. I thought he might have

joined the group or that you had some information about him."

"He might have arrived after I left. Sisters Alice and Barbara, my contacts there, said there were some strange goings-on after Black Peter, that beast, had his showdown with Boy Bishop. Things had really deteriorated. She said that they were all locked in their rooms while Bishop's and Peter's followers were in debate. She said she heard shots, screams and shouting."

"Black Peter. Who is Black Peter?"

"That isn't his real name. His real name is Cudjoe or something like that, but that's not his name either. But when he came to stay with the Nicolaites, he began to read their literature. He became Black Peter, a small dark Spanish page boy who traditionally serves Saint Nicholas. He was some sort of porter. He carried Nicholas's bags. But in some versions, Nicholas carries his bags. There was always a question about who did what for whom. When Boy Bishop left on a fund-raising mission, Black Peter threw a feast and shocked the Nicolaites by unveiling one of his wild paintings. He had removed this oil portrait of Nicholas mounted on a white horse done in the classical European style. Brother James, Boy Bishop's most loyal follower, was furious."

"Nothing in your article mentioned Black Peter."

"Well, my editor cut out the material about Black Peter. He said that people were touchy about stories that featured black men."

"The sixties."

"I don't follow."

"Every time the black man ascends to the scene, America lets its hair down, kicks off its shoes. Its heart goes skinny dipping. Chaos is unsealed."

"Virginia said you were crazy."

"Look," he said, smiling, "are we going to discuss Virginia or are we going to talk about the story?"

"I'm teasing you."

"Maybe I'll have that coffee now." She rose from the couch, smiling; she walked lissomely into the kitchen.

"Black Peter was always kept in the background by Boy Bishop. He didn't want word of Black Peter getting out."

"How did Black Peter and Boy Bishop get together?"

"They became acquainted while Boy Bishop was recruiting prostitutes down on Forty-second Street. Somebody stole Black Peter's dummy, and the dummy was the drawing card for his street hustle. Without his dummy, Black Peter couldn't put on a show. He persuaded Boy Bishop to take him in until he could find a new and bigger dummy. Before you knew it, he had taken over the society and was challenging Boy Bishop's authority. They should never have permitted that nigger to use the library." She returned to the room bearing a silver tray which held two china cups of coffee and a pitcher full of cream.

"You say that Black Peter, or rather Cudjoe, read some literature about this Spanish page. What does that have to do with anything?"

"The legend about Black Peter got his ego all puffed out. He's a short dude, but after coming upon that story he grew ten feet tall and nobody could touch him. He said that he'd come upon evidence which convinced him that Nicholas was Peter's servant and that, this being the case, they should substitute Haile Selassie for the Nicholas ikon. Black Peter should have a master he could respect."

"Where can I find Black Peter?"

"Sister Alice and Barbara say that after the 'reasoning' between the two Nicolaite factions, Boy Bishop and Peter disappeared and Brother Andrew was in charge. It was all a con job, you know. They had some of the most streetwise whores and pimps in New York who'd given up that life to join the Nicolaites, but whores and pimps are sometimes like two-year-olds, especially when they reform. Life to them is a plaything anyway. Why do you think they call themselves players? Notice how whores and pimps get all sentimental around Christmas, buying each other extravagant gifts. What's that song that Nat King Cole sings, where the player promises his prime trick a fur coat, a diamond ring, big Cadillac, and everything?"

"Charles Brown. Merry Christmas, baby, you sure been good to me." Nance was giving away his age. They laughed. "Is there anything else you can tell me about the time you spent doing your story on the Nicolaites?"

"I'd interviewed Brother Andrew and the Sisters Alice and Barbara and was about to interview Brother James, who promised he'd meet me in the garden during the feast where Black Peter was to unveil his painting. Black Peter overheard James and asked me to come to his room on the third floor of the mansion. I didn't see any harm in it. He was the perfect host and brought me some violets and offered me some of his provisions. Some Dragon's Snout and some Dutch schnapps. He had some of his paintings on the wall. He was pretty good. Untrained, but heavy on colors and vision. He couldn't draw, but some of the best painters around can't. Whatever his art lacked in technical craftsmanship, it made up for in originality. He offered me some human-shaped cookies he said he'd baked. Brother James later told me that Black Peter always carried around a cooking pot. And he gave me some candy. The original Black Peter was always either handing out candy or giving people the rod. He was a kidnapper, you know. Took kids into Spain, the naughty ones.

"I realized when I talked with Brother James that bad blood was building up between them. Brother James said he was keeping notes about Black Peter's bad and unruly behavior and was about to recommend his ouster from the group. Brother James didn't feel that he should obey Black Peter's authority. Well, we were walking through the garden and laughing about this and that. Brother James was very close to Boy Bishop. He said that Boy Bishop had always been brilliant and that he had abandoned his class in order to uphold

Nicolaite beliefs. He said that Boy Bishop's father was a big department store executive who lost his fortune when the oil men fired him for not producing huge Christmas sales. He said that the Boy Bishop was out to put Christmas back where it was before big oil moved into the business. His strategy was to infiltrate the establishment and win converts that way. Black Peter had approached him with a wild or crazy scheme. It had something to do with body snatching. He said that Black Peter was a loyal subject before then and used to be the butt of a lot of Boy Bishop's taunts. We were going along and all of a sudden some of Black Peter's people came into the garden. They claimed that Black Peter wanted to know my whereabouts. He'd told them that I was a spy. They grabbed both of us, but not before Brother James hit one of them with a snow-covered stone flower pot. We tried to fight off the others, but there were more of them than there were of us, and so they dragged us before him. He was furious. He jumped up and down on the table and called me all sorts of dirty whore this and that, and he put me out. I was glad to get out. I could hear them arguing as I drove away. I think that Black Peter was going crazy. Brother James said that he had told someone that a water from Tarpon Springs, Florida, was capable of reviving a corpse. He believed in all of Nicholas's miracles, but he wanted Selassie to split off from Nicholas, just as Santa Claus had split off from Nicholas. He saw Nicholas as a model capable of producing endless variations. Those people were really becoming loyal to Peter, especially Brother Andrew, who was beginning to challenge Boy Bishop. They're going to be in for a surprise, because Black Peter isn't from Jamaica at all. He's fake. His name wasn't Cudjoe, either. I looked at his police file. He grew up downtown on Avenue D, in those projects. His first arrest was for stealing a Christmas ham."

Nance looked at his watch. "I better go." She walked him to the door. They focused on each other so long, their eyes bumped.

"Don't let this be your last visit," she said.
"I won't," he said.

19

Zumwalt paced about the hotel ballroom. A bar had been set up and a bartender was dispensing drinks to the reporters who were waiting for the press conference to begin. But where was S.C.? He was late. Some of the assembly were grumbling. Zumwalt whispered to Jack Frost to call S.C.'s room to see what was taking so long. Jack Frost came back and whispered into Zumwalt's ear that there was no response. Zumwalt would have to begin the press conference, hoping that S.C. would soon join him, or else the reporters would leave. They had other stories to file. He decided to go ahead without Santa.

A reporter asked Zumwalt: "Mr. Zumwalt, you've promised the big department store owners that you will be able to triple their sales this year over last year. How, sir, will you manage to do that?"

"Television. Santa is going to do a lot of television. That way, Santa will reach more children. He loves children, you know. I'm sure that you've seen he's more popular than the President, even among the adult population. The department stores will get rid of their inventories in no time." Another reporter raised his hand and was acknowledged.

"Many groups are complaining about the monopoly the North Pole Development Corporation has on Christmas. The poor are saying that they don't get so much as some holly and mistletoe, now that Big North has taken control. They say they can't afford the price of admission charged by the department stores to see Santa."

"That's just the way it is. Don't get me wrong. I would like everybody to be happy. I'd like for everybody to eat a hearty breakfast, have a color TV set and a steak. I'd like everybody to love one another. If it was up to me, everybody would have a million dollars, but that's not the way it works. I didn't set up the rules; I just play by them. Things cost; everything costs; Christmas costs, like everything else."

"Mr. Zumwalt, last evening the First Lady was electrocuted while lighting the White House Christmas tree. What is your reaction to this tragedy, and will this affect Big North's plans for Christmas?" another reporter asked.

"It was a terrible tragedy," Zumwalt said. "But the former—the late First Lady was all for a free market, and I'm sure that she wouldn't want her death to affect the sales inventory ratio. I've sent a telegram to the President expressing my regrets, and I'm sure that I speak for the directors of the North Pole Development Corporation when I say that my heart goes out to the Chief Executive and his family." Jack Frost ran into the room and whispered into Zumwalt's ear.

"Boss, you'd better come outside quick. Santa Claus has gone crazy." Zumwalt ran out and entered the elevator with Jack Frost and his "Floorwalkers," as his men were called; the reporters followed. They got off in the lobby. Crowds of people were milling about, and outside, in the streets, there was a big crowd. Outside, Zumwalt was able to see the source of interest. People were rolling over one another in the streets, leaping and grabbing at the bills that were floating down from Santa's room. Even the staff of the Holiday Inn was outside, grabbing fistfuls of money. Zumwalt and his men ran back into the hotel. They entered the elevator and rose to Santa's floor. They barged into

Santa's room. He was throwing money from a bag to the crowds below. A black man stood next to him. A bellhop? A red carnation was pinned to his lapel. He had an inclination toward the lowly side. Zumwalt grabbed the bag.

"Are you crazy?" Zumwalt grabbed Santa's arm; Santa pulled it away from Zumwalt's grip. Jack Frost and some of the other Floorwalkers rushed Santa, but the little black man came between Santa and the toughs. He flung them about the room as if they were department store mannikins. Jack Frost and his men groggily climbed to their feet. Santa moved into the wingback chair, lit up his long-stemmed pipe, and exhaled. "Fix you a drink?" Santa asked Zumwalt.

"I don't want a drink. Look, who is this guy? What is this nonsense?"

"Get rid of your men and I'll talk." Zumwalt waved the men away; they left the room. Zumwalt sat down.

"We'll talk—what do you mean, we'll talk? This is my room. I'll do the talking and if you don't quit this shit I'm going to call the police. I'm going to fire you. I'm going to—" The bellhop was on the floor, laughing, pounding the floor.

"You sit down," S.C. said to Zumwalt.

"What do you mean, you sit down? Look, I discovered you. Nobody would give you a job. They wouldn't even let you read the weather. You couldn't get a job after punching the producer in the mouth. You were busted, and you read about the job in a newspaper that was lying on the Ping-Pong table in an alcoholic clinic, and you didn't have a dime. I gave you this job, choosing between you and a number of well-qualified candidates—" The bellhop was laughing so hard he began to gasp for breath. ". . . You, what are you laughing at? Why you, you black devil!" Zumwalt started towards the bellhop with his fists balled. The bellhop tripped him by running between his legs.

Zumwalt climbed to his feet, then slumped into a Queen Anne chair.

"Show him the photos," Santa asked the little man. He

went into another room. He came back with a briefcase which was almost as huge as he was. He removed some satin-finished photos and handed them to Santa. Zumwalt's eyes popped when he saw them; he shot up from his seat. He grabbed his forehead. His knees buckled.

"Where did you get these?"

"This is nothing. You ought to see the videotapes," Santa replied.

"I'll do anything you say, under the circumstances. I have no choice."

"Good," Santa said. "I want you to release a statement that I will speak before the Times Square crowds tomorrow; tell them that tomorrow Santa will give them more than the customary Ho Ho Ho." His face a glum mask, Zumwalt started for the door. "O, and one more thing," Santa said. "I want you to clear out of your suite. You can occupy this crummy room." Zumwalt gritted his teeth and left the room. After he closed the door, he could hear the cackling of the little black man.

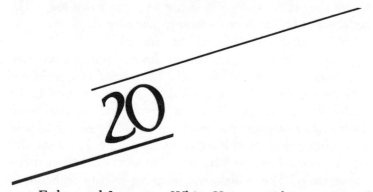

Esther and Joan, two White House maids, encountered each other on the stairway and took the opportunity to get in some gossip.

"John say he heard Mrs. Harding again last night. He said that he recognized that fool woman's old crazy laughter and that it was coming from the room where the President was sitting near his wife's casket. He said that Mrs. Harding was laughin' and starin' down at the dead woman's casket and that the room was glowing in haint light. A green haint light. He said he could see through Mrs. Harding to the snow which was falling outside the window. He say he tried not to look scared and that he just commenced to singing 'Amazing Grace,' and when Mrs. Harding heard that she threw up her bony ghost hands, picked up the hem of that gown she was buried in, and hightailed it back to the land of the duppies," Esther said.

"Po' Miss Harding," Joan said. "She never got over the rumors that she killed her husband for meeting with them fast-lane women around back. What was the President doing while John was dealing with that duppy?"

"He said that the President was asleep and spit was coming down from his lips and that he was holding a half-full glass of whiskey, and he must have had some kind of falling dream because every once in a while he'd jerk his head and then catch himself. Then he stayed quiet a long time and then start to snore."

"The duppies sho' are hopping this Christmas season. One of the downstairs help told me that he was in the kitchen about midnight, having a cup of coffee, and that General Eisenhower came into the kitchen, he almost peed in his pants. He said that Mr. President looked troubled and was begging him to come see about Harry. He said that he was worried about Harry and that he wanted somebody to come and see him. He said that when the general asked him for a cigarette, he just fainted dead away."

"We could have had Social Security if we lived twenty years ago, but now that that's gone, we have to work here until we die, all of those haints be moanin' and clanging on their chains. And that big black ghost-bear that be chasing Andrew Jackson up and down the stairs, Abe Lincoln staring out of the window looking sad, and George Washington crying in the basement."

"My neighbor says that if we took some onions and put them in the corners of each room, and then remove them and then boil for twenty-four hours, those ghosts will go away."

"It would take some pretty strong onions to get rid of the ghosts who live in this house. Besides, do you realize how many rooms are in this house, girl?"

"That was too bad about the First Lady, wasn't it," Esther said.

"Maybe the President will change. Maybe he'll get right, now. He should stay on his knees and ax the Lord for forgiveness the way he's so rough on poor people. Poor John got his grandchile to take care of and he won't even give him a raise."

"I heard the Secretary of Defense and the Secretary of State talking in the Blue Room one day when they were waiting for him to come down and they said they just keep the poor man around for laughs and he didn't have the slightest idea of what was going on in his administration."

"He been in that room for two days with his wife and won't come out. Had the spruce tree burned. I think he going crazy."

"Why did he burn the tree? The tree wasn't guilty. Something happened to the current. They have the F.B.I. looking into the tree's background." They giggle behind their hands.

"White people show is crazy, ain't they?"

"He got John taking him bottles of whiskey up the living quarters, he's been in there drinking day and night and crying at the foot of the casket. When John can't deliver the liquor fast enough, he shouts at John."

"When's John's boy going to get better?"

"Say he might be out of the hospital by Christmas; they had to take off one of the boy's legs."

"You don't mean it?"

"Poor John. First his wife dies, then his two chirren in

that car accident, and now the poor grandchile having his leg problem."

"And the President won't give him a raise. You saw him meeting with those Nazis, didn't you? John spilled a drink on one of those old storm trooper's pants."

"The President's going to end up bad. He's going to torment sure enough, just like the rest of them. That's what Reverend McBee said. Said that the wicked and the powerful will be there doing the dance of unholiness. All of them will have the hotfoot sure enough."

"He broke some of his mirrors last night and was growling."

"Something must be coming over him for him to break the mirrors. He poses in front of that mirror all day. Taking off his clothes and putting them back on. They had to use some floors in Blair House to hold the rest of his wardrobe. They got his shoes down in the basement. I never seen so many shoes."

"He's always in front of a mirror hunching his shoulders, toying with the buttons on his coat, pinching his creases, combing his hair and for him to break one of his precious mirrors—something must be coming over him." A loud moan is heard.

"There he goes now. And something is coming over him."

"I had a dream the other night. It was about the President. I was in some dark foggy section of the city, and I went into this saloon to ask directions and there wasn't no one in the saloon and I heard some moaning and crying coming from the other room and there was all these men and women with little Nazi caps and black leather jackets and black leather pants and they was black leather everywhere and they was rubbing on somebody naked and he was lying on the pool table and they kept on justa rubbing this man who was on the pool table and he was trying to get away and he kept saying let go of me and I tried to get a better look of the man and it was the President, who was naked and he was crying and trying to get away."

"That dream mean somebody going to die. Whenever you dream of somebody naked that means somebody getting ready to go to torment."

21

Zumwalt, Jack Frost, and Zumwalt's bodyguards, the Floorwalkers, sit in S.C.'s old suite. They have plenty of ice. Jack Frost is drinking whiskey and getting meaner by the minute. The TV picture comes on. There are thousands of people in Times Square, curious about what S.C. is going to lay down. A big cheer goes up. They switched to the studio. "What's that, Sandour. . . ?" Realizing that she was on camera, the woman started to speak.

This is billed as a major speech. By Santa Claus. He's now climbing the steps and is approaching his seat on the platform, acknowledging the cheers of the crowd. He is followed by a little black bellboy from the hotel, who is carrying his bags. The Mayor is here to introduce him. This is a very fine moment for the Mayor. Yesterday he rode beside S.C. as he greeted him as he arrived from "Spain," the hacienda owned by a department store magnate. Santa is approaching the speaker's stand.

There's a motley crowd here. Chickens and hustlers from Times Square. Jook Sing gangs from Chinatown, El Barrio, and Harlem. For some reason, this Santa has been able to attract

much of the city's hoodlum element. Low riders, Joe Boys, Yangs,
Fugis, and a number of blue- and purple-haired young women who
have gotten themselves up in lavender mascara and rouge, some of
them are wearing Mohawk haircuts, and there seems to be a lot of
gum-chewing going on. The governor is already on the stand. And
now, ladies and gentlemen, the introduction of Santa for his Times
Square speech which officially gets the Christmas season going.
Usually this speech is made by Oswald Zumwalt, but this year, for
some reason, Santa is making the speech himself, no longer confined
to Ho Ho Ho. Santa Claus is the only major public figure who
doesn't have to sneak around the country like a thief. As anarchist
groups grow in the United States, attacks on public officials have
increased. And now, the Mayor of New York, Kevin Grouch.

"Ladies and gentlemen, I consider it an esteemed honor
and a great privilege to introduce to you a man who brings good
cheer to us all during this Christmas season. A man who can
have the key to this city any time he wants, the key to our
hearts, and isn't it appropriate that the ceremonies occur here
because this is St. Nick's town, the Knickerbocker town. He
has requested this time to make an important speech to us all.
Ladies and gentlemen, our own. Santa Claus." S.C. rises and
starts towards the microphone as a great human cheer goes up.
Doves are set flying. A huge dirigible floats above carrying the
words "Merry Christmas." Balloons rise.

"Thank you, ladies and gentlemen. I consider it a pleasure
to be here with all of you New Yorkers, from the Bronx, from
Queens, from Brooklyn, and from good old Manhattan. I wish
I could delight all of you with candy canes, and fill your
stockings; I'd like to soar above your roofs."

Watching the ceremony on TV, Zumwalt cracks his
knuckles. He is beginning to sweat. Jack Frost shoots up from
his seat and looks to Zumwalt, and to the Floorwalkers, for an
explanation.

"I think it's time to have a grown-up Christmas, children of all ages. A Christmas where we can get to the bottom of things. Get to the bottom of what's troubling this country so. This is no time for animal crackers and gingerbread." Jack Frost shakes his fist at the set.

"What's wrong with him? What is he saying? Should we plug him?"

"Let him go," Zumwalt says. "I'll explain later."

Warming to his subject, Santa begins to pace up and down the platform, his hands clasped behind his back. He tugs at his beard and a tongue-in-cheek grin comes over his face. Nobody stirs in the crowd. All you can hear is an occasional police horse's hoof clop against the sidewalk. The motor of a small plane buzzes overhead. Times Square stands still as in one of those last-day films, the city frozen, people clogging up the exits from the city in an attempt to escape the monster.

He continues slowly, tentatively. "On the way over here I was thinking of an appropriate metaphor with which to describe this cold famine of the spirit which is afflicting those of us who reside in this wonderful Northern Hemisphere, these cold winters, and what has been described as the cold, mean mood of the country. I've thought about what made us what we are today, a nation of Scrooges. And I thought back to the beginning of these cold, blue winters, that long winter of 1980 which began America's long Christmas blues. Every year, as you have seen, the season gets colder and more heartless, and whole families perish in tenement fires. Every year the American dead wander about a little more restless, and the days grow short. They wander about in the day as well as the night, all those brave people who spoke out, emerging from the cemeteries: The lynched, the shot, the martyred.

"I look at France, weeping to melancholy violins, England getting tanner each summer, Berlin a permanent beige, Amsterdam butterscotch, and of course the browning of Paris, Spain darker than usual, and I think of this nation of lonely people, of lonely alienated male assassins alone in their motel rooms, hamburger wrappings scattered about, empty ice cream cartons in with the rubbish, people alienated from the past, the future, nature, and one another. And how did we get that way, and what is wrong with us? We scream and kick and say no when we can't get our way. We say no to the sick, no to the destitute. We say no to the millions of refugees now crowding our cities, tired, jobless, hungry, using garbage-can lids for pillows. And the little children searching for discarded cans or bottles, wearing ragged sneakers in the snow, and I keep thinking of a two-year-old when I think of an appropriate metaphor with which to describe this sour, Scroogelike attitude which began with the Scrooge Christmas of '80. Ladies and gentlemen, boys and girls, The President, whose Secret Service code name was Rawhide, had been elected and a mood of grouchiness and bitchiness swept the land, as cold as the Arctic winds, but it wasn't half as cruel as what was to come.

"Two years old, that's what we are, emotionally—America, always wanting someone to hand us some ice cream, always complaining, Santa didn't bring me this and why didn't Santa bring me that." People in the crowd chuckle. "Nobody can reason with us. Nobody can tell us anything. Millions of people are staggering about and passing out in the snow and we say that's tough. We say too bad to the children who don't have milk. I weep as I read these letters the poor children send to me at my temporary home in Alaska.

"And where are the eggs, and the apples, and the oranges? Where is the milk? I'll tell you where they are, rotting in warehouses and on lake embankments. Rotting. The grain is rotting unused." Santa pauses to look over his shoulder at the politicians who sit on the platform.

The Governor is frowning like a distempered bear. The Mayor is trying to laugh the whole thing off, but he is getting nervous too. His Tartar blood is rising and he is more than a little mad. Santa Claus continues. "Look at all of the people homeless, wandering the streets. Suppose one of them was Jesus Christ. Would you say no to Jesus Christ? Would you lock the door of the church and freeze the Lord out?"

Santa turns to the murmuring dignitaries who are sharing the speaker's stand. He turned around and pointed to the Mayor. "Do you know what the Mayor would do if Jesus Christ came to Gracie Mansion and asked for some Christmas cheer? The Mayor would probably have the Lord deloused and thrown in the Tombs. The Mayor is eating. Look at him, a bald-head, fat as a rich ball of butter. Got a head like a bald-headed turtle. He had dinner with the Rockefellers last night up at Asia House. We got hold of the menu from one of the waiters inside. Let me read it to you." Santa put on his spectacles. The Mayor is livid. "Cold Gaspé salmon, roast fillet of beef with roast potatoes, and vanilla ring with black cherries."

The Mayor gets up and tries to wrest the menu from Santa Claus but Santa puts his hands on his hips and bumps the Mayor into the audience with his belly. The Mayor is carried to the street by the hoodlums, and when he comes up he is tattered, his jacket missing and one shoe off. He is rescued by some policemen. The Governor scrambles off the stand and is rushed from the scene by a speeding limousine, leaving the other dignitaries to fend for themselves. Some police are trying to get to Santa, but the crowd blocks their way, and other mounted policemen begin to move into the crowd; screaming begins. "I know what they're going to say," Santa shouts, "they're going to say that Santa is crazy. Do you think Santa is crazy?" The crowd yells no. "They're going to say that Santa is out of his mind. Do you think that Santa is out of his mind?" The crowd yells "No!" "I say they're the ones who are crazy. There is now a nuclear bomb for every man, woman, and child in the country; in other words, ladies and gentlemen, boys and girls, each person has a personal nuclear weapon, and this situation exists after what happened in South Carolina. When will they learn? I say we fight the people who destroyed the

Adirondack lakes, the New Jersey shore, and Niagara Falls. I say it's time to fight the people who rob us in the supermarket and give our children slow, agonizing leukemia death. I say it's about time to fight the people who gave us acid rain, fight the people who destroyed the ozone belt, and the carbon dioxide excreters whose wastes will soon cause the oceans to rise twenty feet. Do you know who owns Christmas as well as just about every other holiday in this country? The oil men. Not only do they own the department stores, but they're buying up all the copper, lead, and zinc as well. How many of you can live the life that the rich of this country lead? How many of you have dined with Brooke Astor? How many of you have gone skiing at Aspen, Sun Valley, Klosters, Zermatt, Gstaad? How many of you can buy your clothes at Adolfo's or Oscar de la Renta's, or how many of you have had brunch at the Four Seasons or have eaten chopped liver and strawberry cheesecake at Mel Krupin's, or have had your hair done by Monsieur Marc, your face done by Manzoni? I say it's time to pull these naughty people off their high chairs and get them to clean up their own shit. Let's hit them where it hurts, ladies and gentlemen. In their pockets. Let's stop buying their war toys, their teddy bears, their dolls, tractors, wagons, their video games, their trees. Trees belong in the forest." Before Santa can continue, a huge cheer goes up and people start chanting, "Boycott! Boycott! Boycott!" and some of the gang members help him down before the police can stop his speech. Fist fights break out between supporters of Santa and his opponents in the audience. The gangs are battling the police with their chains and blackjacks. The police are cracking heads left and right. The whole area before the speaker's stand begins to take on the appearance of a hockey game.

22

A string quartet from the Marine Band was playing some sad music, the kind the Germans call *Traurig*. The spruce tree burned, sending sparks into the black Washington sky. In the park across the street from the White House, the President stood, watching the old tree go down. He'd knocked down quite a few and stood there, reeling in the snow. He wore an overcoat over his pajamas. He needed a shave and he hadn't bathed for awhile or looked at himself in the mirror. After the tree had become ashes, the President dismissed the string quartet and headed back to the White House, and the room where his wife lay in state. She had been so badly burned that they had to keep the coffin closed. The civil service employees and the White House staff and children had watched in horror as the First Lady fried and sizzled down to fat. They were helpless to do anything about it. "God! God!" the President cried, shaking his fist towards the falling snow. "Who will do all the handshaking? Who will see to it that my socks are packed? Who will listen to the drafts of my speeches and rub my back until I fall asleep? Who will see to it that the Rose Garden is trimmed and that there are three hundred places set for a state dinner? Who will take charge of the Easter Egg hunt? And suppose I have to make a decision affecting the future course of human generations to come? Who will make it for me?"

He sat in the room in which the coffin had been placed, sobbing and drinking the refills his faithful White House butler John kept bringing. The room began to move. The President's head began to whirl. He thought he heard the tinkle of a little bell; it was delicate, almost inaudible, still he thought he heard it. There, standing before him, was a black-bearded ascetic-appearing man. He was elderly and his narrow face had an olive complexion. He was wearing a gown, a long cloak covered with equilateral crosses, sandals, and a long Bishop's hat. He walked with the support of a staff. On his chest he wore the Star of David. The man had a nervous habit. He held three tiny gold balls in his fist, and he was constantly squeezing them.

23

He had that wet look all right. Reverend Clement Jones was as greased as a pig and was wearing a suit that must have cost about eight hundred dollars. Admiral Lionel Matthews sat, tight-lipped, formal, banging his hand slowly against a table. He couldn't conceal his rage as he watched different television sets, set up in the Oval Office, broadcasting reaction to Santa's speech. The young hoodlums who were devoted to Santa Claus could be seen running through the streets, setting fires and overturning cars, not only in the United States but elsewhere in the world. They wore their faces painted in a manner that used to be acceptable only in the *National Geographic*, confirming for Lionel Matthews, Reverend Jones, and the King of Beer,

Robert Reynolds, that these indeed were the last days of the West, unless true patriots put their feet down. Mobs roamed the area about Holiday Inn, and some placed flowers at the entrance to the hotel where Santa was staying. Some of the dreads had the crowd swaying as they played their haunting renditions of "Santa Claus Is Coming to Town."

Bob Krantz was on the phone obtaining information about the situation as Reverend Jones, the Admiral, and the King of Beer Robert Reynolds were discussing the scene that the networks and cable were broadcasting. "It's all the wimmin's fault," said Reverend Jones. "They refused to yield their wombs to the Lord's plans during the sixties and the seventies. They refused to remain home nesting, but took leave of their God-ordained role and went out there to try to mix it up with men. And now their chirren are upon us in the 1990s. Chirren they abandoned as they sought to 'find themselves.' St. John warned us about Santa Claus, he warns against the Nicolaites, chapter two, verse six, the Book of Revelations."

"That's all very interesting," the Admiral said, "but I think they ought to let me handle this Santa Claus business. Bible quoting and TV preaching doesn't seem to be affecting the matter, if you ask me."

"Maybe we ought to have Bob ring the Governor of New York and advise him on how to handle this Santa Claus business. Have him send in the guard. The local New York police can't seem to handle it," the King of Beer Robert Reynolds said.

"He won't do anything about it. He's one of the leaders of the forces of the Antichrist," Reverend Jones said. "Wish the Rock was here. He'd know what to do. Never will forget the day we got the news from Attica. I was in the middle of a sermon when one of the deacons told me. I felt proud of being an American that day."

"Me too," said the Admiral. "That Rock. What a way to go, too, huh," the Admiral said, nudging and winking at his companions. "Said he was so wrapped up in those two women that the emergency squad had to take a crowbar to pry them loose, and the black gal, she—"

"Was it true that he brought the bloody and brain-smeared clothing from the prison up to his estate at Pocantico Hills, placed them in a seldom-used Japanese bedroom, stripped and wallowed about in them?" asked the King of Beer. Bob Krantz put down the telephone receiver before anybody could answer. The men trained their eyes on him.

"Goddamnit, the interest rates have shot so high that you need binoculars to see them. Three department store executives have jumped from their windows and millions of youngsters have put pressure on their parents to follow the Christmas boycott that Santa requested. If it weren't enough that we have these world crises heating up, Santa Claus has to go and blow his stack. Some of the protestors are lying down in front of Christmas tree shipments. I've ordered that future shipments be sent with an armed guard escort," Krantz announced.

"Why don't you arrest him?" the Admiral demanded.

"Arrest who?" Krantz asked, wearily placing his glasses on the desk.

"Arrest Santa Claus," the King of Beer said.

"Be serious, gentlemen."

"Now look here, Krantz," Reverend Jones said. "We put you in power, and don't forget how the Lord gave me the power to lift that car off you. We demand that you do something about Santa Claus."

"I'm sorry," Krantz said. "I haven't gotten much sleep. I'll try to figure something out."

"You ought to let me have one of those nuclear submarines," the Admiral said. "I'd surround the Holiday Inn and make Santa Claus come out and surrender."

"That's not a good idea," the King of Beer said. "The last time you manned a nuclear submarine you were eighty years old and you rammed it into the West Coast. Remember? There are some members of Congress who'd crow our ears off if they knew that you were up here in the Oval Office giving advice. Besides, you'd have to bring the sub into New York Harbor before you could surround the Holiday Inn with it."

The Admiral stared at his shoes.

"Gentlemen, don't worry. Kevin Grouch, the Mayor of New York, says that he has the whole thing under control."

"Are you sure that you can trust him, Krantz?" Reverend Jones asked. "He and his Yid buddies might be behind the whole thing if you ask me. I mean, which race of people would rejoice the most if Christmas was ruined?"

"Good point," the King of Beer said.

"I'm always impressed by your scholarship, Reverend," the Admiral said.

"Incidentally, Krantz, what's the status of Operation Two Birds?" the King of Beer asked.

"The countdown begins tomorrow," Krantz answered. "Next week we'll advise the top-rate vitals to leave the target cities."

"I have to get back to Colorado," the King of Beer said.

"How's the fight with the Injuns coming?" Reverend Jones asked.

"My family has been making beer since they came through the Cumberland Pass with Dan Boone. They shot Injuns alongside Mordecai Lincoln and joined old Andy Jackson in his war against the Seminoles. Injuns come and Injuns go, but Regal Beer is here for an eternity." The King of Beer picked up his stetson, shook hands with the other three, and, spurs jangling, left the Oval Office. The Admiral and Reverend Jones and Krantz rose. The Admiral put on his Napoleon hat, and Reverend Jones, his coat.

"How's business?" the Admiral asked the Reverend.

"Pretty good," the Reverend responded. "Opened a few more mail-order colleges last week. Prayed for the sick, and warned the wicked. Krantz, you're doing a good job," Reverend Jones said. The Admiral nodded.

"I owe it all to you. You, the Admiral, and the King of Beer. I guess I'd still be working for Babylonian television were it not for your intervention, Reverend Jones."

"That wasn't me, that was the Lord, son. The Lord's advice is worth more than ours. Never forget that, son."

"I don't," said Bob Krantz. "I speak to the Lord day and night."

"Good boy," the Admiral said. "Stay on your knees. That's the best position for running the state." The two men pumped his hands and left. Relieved, Bob Krantz leaned back into his chair and lit a cigarette. Cigarettes were his only remaining vice.

He'd stopped drinking and snorting coke a few years before, but whenever those three dropped by the White House—they always "just happened to be in the neighborhood"—he couldn't conduct the business of state without them sitting around, offering ridiculous advice on anything that came to mind. The Reverend went about each day warning of the Second Coming; the Admiral sometimes wandered through Washington streets without the slightest idea of where he was; the King of Beer was a bore with his strange obsessions and his "injun"-hating.

Just as he had asked the press to begin building up resentment against a strange and foreign power, here comes Santa Claus to foul things up by removing the war hysteria from page one. What had come over Santa Claus? All he had uttered in the past was ho ho ho, but now he was given to inflammatory, polemical rhetoric, ranting diatribes, and stale invective.

Krantz put on his coat and began to head from the Oval Office to his apartment in the Watergate complex. What had really frightened him was the Attorney General's conclusion that he didn't have enough manpower to quell the disturbances taking place in New York. But soon New York's agony would be over, and if Santa happened to remain behind after Christmas Day, there would be no more him, either. He wondered was he doing the right thing. Would Christ do what he was doing were Christ in his place? He turned out the light, and walked down the hall.

I know it's going to hurt people but we must think of future generations in this country. Though I wouldn't want anybody confusing my views with those of Reverend Jones, he's right in a way. The Gussack race has been pushed around. Why, if we hadn't escaped across the land barrier connecting Africa to Europe there wouldn't even be any of us. The ice age saved us. And then look at all of the things we've given to the world. Christianity, music and art—and now they're surrounding us. What would anybody do? Christ would want us to do the right thing. What would happen to his religion if we weren't taking this step? Yes, dear Savior, I'm doing the right thing, Krantz thought.

So overcome by the spirit, Bob Krantz dropped to his knees. He removed his glasses. "Heavenly Father, I come before you with a great burden. Thou came to me when Reverend Jones lifted the wheels from my body. Thou helped me during the long months of convalescence, and I vowed that I would be Thy humble servant. It was Thee who told me that I should take the job as Dean Clift's presidential aide after the Colorado gang offered it to me. It was Thee who told me to push through Operation Two Birds, a plan to save all of Thy Christian work from being overrun by the forces of the Anti-Christ, Thou sayest, sweet Jesus.

"They congratulated me on Operation Two Birds, Lord, because they didn't know that it was Thy plan, and that Thou had brought it to me, as the instrument for Thy desires. Lord, I'm beginning to have doubts about this plan, I mean, won't a lot of people get hurt, Lord? I'm asking you to relieve me of my doubts, sweet Jesus. I am asking Thee to send me a sign that Operation Two Birds is the right thing to do." He rose. The long hall was dark. He heard some heavy breathing down at the other end. He began to sweat and slowly trot towards the exit.

He heard some growling. He looked behind him and some hairy, red-eyed thing was galloping towards him on all fours. He ran until he was safely outside the White House and underneath the moonlight. He looked back. Nothing was there.

24

Vixen hadn't stopped crying since she heard Santa's speech. She knew now why she'd always go into flushes when the former soap-opera star was behind her at the water cooler, or passed her in the hall. He had been beaten by Bob Krantz, beaten by Zumwalt, and his bodyguards, and seemed to have an overall Hegelian victim thing with people, but now she'd discovered the real man underneath all the paint and white dye. She had been through eight or so American men, and they'd all turned out to be mama's boys. Competitors for the Great Teat whose conversations revolved around themselves. Bully the blacks, bully the women. Machotots. Santa had shown himself to be different from the other self-centered knaves who pulled her pigtails in grammar school, went too far in the back seat of the car in high school, and leaned on her in every relationship. And Sam. The biggest disappointment of them all. From the day her marriage broke up to the present, she'd gone through some relationships only because she was too embarrassed to go into a store to buy a dildo or vibrator. New England, she guessed. She tried a "sexual preference" relationship, but all her partner talked about was how awful men were. She talked about it so often one could conclude that what she really wanted was a man, but that can't be true because Freud was a patriarch. There was no answer as to why her "sexual preference" roommate always talked about men.

But now that she knew that she loved Santa, she was ready for a meaningful relationship. She wasn't political but she had always envied her mother for coming to maturity in the sixties when the Celtic-African visionaries walked the land, M.L.K., J.F.K., and R.F.K. Days of thunder and days of drums. Brave hearts exploding like tropical flowers. "The Impossible Dream" and "Bridge Over Troubled Water." And then the blue seventies and the cold eighties. Santa, of all people. The only voice that hadn't become as jaded as Ann Sheridan in *Juke Girl* (1942) in which a young actor named Ronald Reagan organized the lettuce workers against the bosses. The only compassionate voice in a Scroogelike country, the kissing cousin of South Africa. She always thought that her mother was a dizzy hippie with that silly Billie Holiday gardenia over her ear, and the Dorothy Lamour sarong. But now, Santa had won *her!* She knew that she could do something to help people. She knew where her place was: near Santa Claus. Her heart was thumping rapidly with excitement; her palms were sweating. How had he put it? The Terrible Twos. The right metaphor for this affliction. She always complained about not having enough. She always felt she needed more. She knew that for families in South America, her four bedrooms, two baths, and huge living room and parlor would seem like a villa. She knew that under the Dutch, in what the Dutch called South Africa, whole black families lived in one room.

And now Santa had spoken out. Spoken out against the consumption and greed. She wanted somebody like Santa. He had what the Japanese called *Yamato Damashi*. He was thoughtful and reflective, unlike some of the men she knew who were always standing before a pinball machine, or shooting bears. That's all Alaskan men seemed to enjoy doing. That reminded her. She would get rid of her black bear coat. She would sell her three thousand dollars' worth of dresses. She would get rid of her Lincoln. She would shove herself from her high chair and stop behaving like a daddy's girl. She would help Santa fight the powerful people his speech would surely offend. She finished packing her luggage. Now she had to confirm her plane reservations. She'd scribble a note to Flinch Savvage, or Sav-váge as he pronounced it. He was sweet. If only he didn't have a drinking problem. She removed some pink, scented stationery from her desk and began to hurriedly scribble. She was interrupted by Blitz, Santa's helper who was now on loan to her.

"Sorry to disturb you, Madame, but Master Savvage is here."

"Tell him I'm busy, Blitz."

"Yes, Madame." But as Blitz turned to the door, Flinch Savvage forced his way in. "Why haven't you answered my calls, I knew you were home." He staggered about the room. He knocked over a lamp.

"I'll take care of this," she said, dismissing Blitz.

"I bought a couple of tickets to the Ice Capades, thought we could have dinner and then—"

"You're drunk."

"I've only had about two beers."

"You know that you can't drink. It makes you crazy."

"Gimmie a kiss." He stumbled towards her, she side-stepped, and he fell against the dresser.

"Look, you may as well know, I'm leaving for New York. I'm going to join Santa Claus." She was adjusting an earring.

"You what?"

"I told you that I'm going to join Santa Claus. He needs me." He grabbed her arm.

"Stop, you're hurting me."

"I won't let you go."

"You haven't the power to stop me. I'm in love with him."

"You love him. When's the last time you looked at his waistline?"

"That's all you think about. Your body. Your education. The right kind of aftershave lotion. What good is it? They use you against your own people. Besides, you're a lousy lover. So inhibited. Afraid to experiment. Afraid to do what I want."

"That's not what you were saying the other night." He grabbed her roughly to him.

"Let me go," she screamed. Blitz rushed in. Savvage picked up Blitz's mangled and distorted body and threw it against the wall. She was hysterical. "Now you've proven that you're a man." She laughed, scornfully.

"Vixen, I—"

"Get out."

Savvage started for the door. He looked to her and then to Blitz, whom she was helping to his feet. Savvage left.

25

The colonial-style table was covered with bottles of tranquilizers and whiskey. While the President's physical self sat in a dark blue bathrobe monogrammed with the Presidential seal, his spirit-plasm flew hand in hand with St. Nicholas, out the window, and soaring above the Treasury Department building, the Taft Monument, the Washington Monument, the J. Edgar Hoover Memorial Building. The President lost consciousness and came to, riding with St. Nicholas in an elevator. Its walls and floor were painted white. He didn't know what to make of it. Noticing his confusion, St. Nicholas said, "We're on the way to the American hell, so hold on, it's quite a place. You know that the hell of Dante, and the hell of the Bible are uncomfortable, but you ain't seen nothing yet," he said, as they flew into Kentucky's Mammoth Cave. "The American hell is a hell of roving duppies, Hopi two hearts, witches, warlocks, Bruhas, and all manner of evil spirits which can change shape as much as they wish."

"Why the elevator?" Clift asked, as they approached an elevator located inside the Cave surrounded by the rock.

"Because it was the elevator that made the United States, at one time, the most powerful capitalistic country in the world, because without elevators you couldn't have skyscrapers. And so in the elevator we go from world to world, an elevator that never gets stuck between worlds. In the American hell there are ten worlds." The elevator stopped. "This is the first world," St. Nicholas said. The elevator opened on what seemed to be a hospital floor, but the rooms had bars on the windows. Out of his peripheral vision, the President was sure he saw an animal in a white smock dash by. He appeared to be a wolf or a coyote, and he ran swiftly through the corridor.

"Don't worry about them. Don't let them get you. They won't strike unless you strike first," the Saint said. They walked into the waiting room and there, leafing through a 1940s issue of *Life* magazine, was a man he recognized from his shining army black shoes and his beige pants and the jacket he made famous. When the figure spoke, he sounded as if he were speaking under water or choking on bubbles. He noticed the President and then the Saint, got up, and approached him excitedly. "At last you came, you came." The President turned to Saint Nicholas, who merely smiled and rolled the three gold balls nervously about in his hands.

"I tried to get Sherman to come," the figure said. "Sherman used to be my right hand. I'm lost without him. He'd take care of things while I went out to play golf with Freeman Gosden and Charles Correll. Those fellows used to keep me in stitches. Sherman would look after all of the details but Sherman seems to be only interested in maple syrup and zucchini marmalade where he is up in New Hampshire. Can't say I blame him. But what's important is that you came to see about Harry.

"Harry's behind that wall there," the figure said, pointing. "Those doctors who come and give him his pills say they're doctors, but they look like coyotes to me, and those pills, every time he takes those pills he seems to get worse." A black dog entered the room, red-eyed, baring its teeth. The figure put its hand at its sides as straight as arrows. The dog sniffed the figure's trousers, turned around and trotted out of the room.

"He's one of the guards," the figure said. "Here, come see about Harry." Nicholas and Dean Clift followed the figure to a barred window through which he could see a short man wearing a straw hat, double-breasted suit, bow tie, and white loafers. He was walking briskly up and down the room using a cane for support.

"He walks up and down because he doesn't want to go to sleep. He says that when he tries to sleep he dreams of Japanese faces, burnt, twisted, and peeling, with no eyeballs. It was the generals and scientists who made him do it. Harry never thought much of himself, that's why he swore all the time. He was intimidated by scientists and generals just as I was always impressed by the top-rate vitals of big business, and so when they told him that they wanted him to drop little man and big man on those Japanese cities he gave his ok. What did he know about physics? How did he know that the people who were wounded would carry that white flash in their genes and that dozens of deformed generations would be born? It was just supposed to be a war, not judgment. That was no military act, that was an insult to nature and to God. Harry Truman is the most tormented and alienated person down here. The nightmare followed him beyond the grave."

Dean Clift couldn't believe what the General told him. Harry Truman? That gutsy spunky haberdasher from Missouri? The populist? The one who stood up to General Douglas MacArthur? What was harder to understand was why the General was there. The World War II General who had become such a grandfather image to America of the 1950s. What was he doing here? Where did he go wrong?

St. Nicholas put his fingers to his lips.

The General pulled a Camel from a pack of cigarettes.

"I know what you're thinking. What am I doing here? Why aren't I on another floor? Me. Who is the father even to Walter Cronkite. Doug MacArthur told me that I could have been the second messiah. He was on his knees saying Ike, Ike, you could be the second messiah. He wanted me to put a nuclear field in the Yalu River, he said. Up on Morningside Heights. I was president of Columbia then, and they didn't have much for me to do, and so I used to invite all of the old war buddies over and we'd swap war stories. But I know that you're still wondering why I'm here. Come over here." They followed the old man to a window in the land of Diddie Wah Diddie, sometimes cold, sometimes hot, depends upon the floor you go to, sometimes city, sometimes desert with the coyotes flying above the cactus and the rattlesnakes.

Coyotes with the wings of long-extinct reptiles.

The Saint stood behind them in the shadows which were the color of blue they use on Spanish television horror movies. Dwight Eisenhower was standing at the window looking down at the Congo jungle scene that had materialized below. A primitive rural road was nearly hidden by large clumps of bush. Dean Clift was watching, watching the pitiful, weary old spirit as he sadly kept his attention riveted to the road, and while studying the General he thought of Chuck Berry, the Coasters,

Fats Domino, Arthur Godfrey, Debbie Reynolds, and Eddie Fisher, 3-D movies, and the Kefauver committee. Suddenly, a black Citroen pulled up and a body was shoved out. It owned a bloody, contorted, intellectual-looking face, scholarly mustache and goatee, and a poet's eyes underneath a startling black pompadour. The ghost from Abilene, Texas, began to wail and grieve.

"If it hadn't been for Dulles," he cried. "That man had so much Bible and brimstone inside of him. The whole family—everybody but Allen was like him. They even had a fidgety woman preacher in the family. Dulles became haunted by that young black man. Said that when the young man, then a new leader of the Congo, visited Washington he sassed Dillon and the others. Swore up and down that Lumumba would bring the Communists to the Congo. Said that the Communism was the bitch of Babylon. Kept it up. Kept it up so much that I started smoking again, though I had sworn off the habit. And so one day, I was anxious to get out and play a couple of rounds of golf at Burning Tree and they'd been pestering me all day about this Patrice Lumumba fellow, and so I stamped my foot and said, a guy like that ought to take a hike. I should have known when they started shaking hands and congratulating each other that something was up. I didn't mean for them to go and kill the man.

"I always wondered how it would have turned out if I hadn't relied so much on the people around me. I said to myself, Ike, you got it made. You rose from an obscure soldier to the pinnacle of military power. I didn't want to blow it all by being President. I didn't want to rock the boat during those eight years. So I delegated responsibility. Maybe I could have become the second messiah as Douglas said. But, I guess I can't really complain. This place is a country club in comparison to the people down in the tenth world. I hear they have spirit-eating cannibals down there who are on the prowl for fresh ghost meat."

The laughter could be heard coming from inside the Citroen. The corpse of the Congo leader, its hands tied behind its back, lay face down in the dirt. The Saint informed Dean Clift, who was close to tears, that they had to leave.

"Got to go?" the old soldier said. "Well, it's pretty decent of you young fellows to come down and see about Harry and me. And that part about not losing a night's sleep over the damage done by little man and big man. Don't believe a word of it. Harry cried in Justice Douglas's arms. And you know what happened to the young man who flew the B-52 plane? He went crazy, you know." He started to wave as Nicholas and Dean Clift left for the elevator. "Hold on a minute." They turned to see the General trying to catch up with them.

"That Atlas nose cone. You know the one they put up into space? They made a tape of my voice and put it inside the nose cone. Is that Atlas still flying around the globe?" Saint Nicholas assured the spirit that indeed the Atlas was still flying and that he had passed it flying to Washington.

The old soldier paused again before vanishing into the mist. "You know," he said, "I don't know what I miss more, Mamie or the quail hash she used to make. She never complained. The perfect Army wife. You know, we moved twenty-seven times. That's what I remember about that woman—hanging up and taking down drapes. She got so that she could fill out a change-of-address card in ten seconds flat."

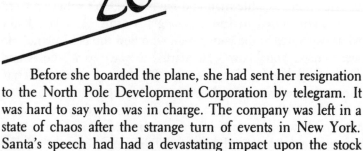

26

Before she boarded the plane, she had sent her resignation to the North Pole Development Corporation by telegram. It was hard to say who was in charge. The company was left in a state of chaos after the strange turn of events in New York. Santa's speech had had a devastating impact upon the stock market, frankincense and myrrh were taking one hell of a beating. Conflict had broken out between Santa's supporters, mostly young, and Santa's detractors, mostly old.

After the flight from the West Coast to La Guardia, Vixen had successfully hailed a cab for the trip downtown to the Holiday Inn.

"Why all the traffic, driver?"

"You must not have heard the news, ma'am."

"I just got in from Alaska, we don't get much from the outside world where I'm living, and there is only one TV channel, something about mountain interference with the signals."

"Santa Claus and some of the young toughs who've taken up with him, some really tough schoolboys, had some kind of ceremony in Flushing. There were motorcycles and cars everywhere. There's a church up there that's supposed to have the hair and a piece of skull from the original Saint Nicholas. I'm telling you, Christmas isn't the same since I was a kid. It's become real complicated. I mean I'm all for free enterprise and against Communism, and so I didn't oppose it when this fellow, Oswald Zumwalt, bought the rights to Santa Claus, but this season they've taken it too far. Why, some of these juveniles were arrested for taking their family jewels and money to Santa Claus at the Holiday Inn. They had baskets and bags of loot for him. And the students have taken up outside the hotel. Roughing up passersby who say something bad about Santa Claus. And that speech he made. Out-and-out socialism. Now I understand why he wears red."

Vixen crossed her legs and the cab driver glanced at her knees through the rearview mirror. He studied her. No, it couldn't be. She looked at him through the mirror. "Anything wrong, driver?" she asked. She frowned. She looked at the picture and name on his license.

"Sam?"

"Vixen? Vixen, I thought I'd never see you again. All I had was your note. It's been years."

"I live in Alaska now."

"Yes, I remember. You've been in the newspaper, you work for the company that's marketing Santa Claus."

"Yes. What are you doing with yourself?"

"O, married. I have two kids. We live in Hoboken, across the river."

"Still painting?"

"Not as much as I used to. Just don't have any more time. I teach classes at Pratt and drive the car at night. It's really expensive supporting a family and teaching. You have any kids?"

"No, I never married, Sam. I just didn't think that child-rearing and a career mixed."

"I know what you mean. We have this two-year-old. She always wants to eat daddy's drumstick and sit in daddy's chair. I let her have her way but it's pretty tough, you know; I was the one who always had the drumstick and now I fight with a two-year-old over it. You know how two-year-olds are. Their plates will be full but they'll have their eyes on everybody else's plates, or they'll have a cookie in their hand and yet ask for another cookie, or the whole bag of cookies."

"You look very good, Sam."

"I try to take care of myself. Had a heart attack a couple of years ago, but now I'm watching the old waistline."

"What happened to Romeo?"

Sam studied her in the mirror. Their eyes met for a moment. "O, he's doing fine. He's running an ad firm in Los Angeles and has bought a condominium." The car reached the Holiday Inn. The scene was bedlam. Crowds had gathered in front of the hotel to catch a glimpse of Santa. Youth gang members, some wearing white berets, scanned the crowd; some stood on rooftops.

27

James Providence and Luke Charity, two Indians who worked in the mail-order room of the Big North, were drinking some kind of Canadian ale, relaxing in a bar many of the employees of Big North frequented. They were wearing plaid shirts, denims, and boots. They were staring at the scene at the bar from the table where they sat.

"I never did like him. What is he doing in this bar anyway, drinking with us?"

"What do you think it's all about?" said Luke.

"Who knows. Everything is uncertain. I hear that the Japanese bank has had to give Big North a loan so that they can meet the payroll." The headlines on the newspaper that lay next to James's elbow read, "Santa No Longer Jolly." The caption under Santa's picture, taken during the Times Square Rally, read, "Says No More Ho Hos."

"When I went home last night and the wife said that Santa had made that speech, I was nearly knocked on the seat of my pants. That guy, I thought. The meekest, most pushed-around guy you'd ever want to meet."

"Well, he certainly did turn the tables on them. I'd love to see that Oswald Zumwalt's face."

"What do you suppose it all means?"

"Beats me. There's talk of a strike. I've even heard that Big North is going to be sold. The lobby was full of creditors this morning. Nobody has been able to reach Zumwalt. It's OK with me. My kid said this morning that he didn't want anything for Christmas. The wife too. They heard Santa's speech and agreed with him."

"I got the same thing over at my house. The kids said they were going to stick with Santa. That these bad men he was talking about ought to get the rod for being naughty." The men laughed. Suddenly, there was the sound of broken glass. The men looked up. Flinch Savvage was leaning over the bar. He started quarreling with the bartender, demanding more drink.

"How long do you think they're going to let him stay in here, carrying on that way?"

"The bartender can't do anything. Flinch has pull with the company." Luke leaned over and whispered to James. "I hear he's diddling that Gussuck girl, Vixen."

"How do you know that Flinch is getting it?"

"My sister works up at the ski lodge. She says that Flinch and the woman are there quite often." Flinch tried to punch a man standing next to him. He missed and landed on the floor. He got up, brushed himself off, and returned to his drink.

"Jesus, do you think he's going to be able to find his way home?"

"Who cares. He never cared for us Indians. Remember how he used to be such a goody-two-shoes. Sucking up to the nuns."

"I never did like him."

"You shouldn't be so hard. He used to go hunting with us. Was a good shot. Used to bag a lot of deer. Then he went away to the white man's college. He changed."

"Maybe you're right. He did try to save the old chief from jail."

"Yeah, but they jailed him anyway. He died there, but then the tree got even. The tree picked a life to make up for the chief's. That was a mean old tree with a nasty temper. It didn't want to be disturbed. No ravens would go near it." There was a crash. Some of the other Indians lifted Savvage to his feet. He staggered, and shoved the Indians away from him. He said something like "Goddamn Indians."

"Boy, anybody else would have been thrown out of here an hour ago."

"They're afraid of that Vixen. She's right up there next to Zumwalt. Arctic woman. You remember Manny? She fired Manny because she was walking through the hall one day and she thought she heard him mumble 'that bitch.' Manny had three kids to support. She made it so that he couldn't find another job in town."

Flinch Savvage finally left the tavern. He staggered down the deserted, sleet-covered streets toward his car. It was teeth-chattering cold. He was humming a chorus from "Rudolph, the Red-Nosed Reindeer," about one of the famous antlered animals introduced to Alaska by Sheldon Jackson, the missionary who brought them from Siberia. "Serves the bitch right. She and her fat bastard deserve each other. She'll come back after she finds out that he was drunk when he made that speech. That's probably what happened. He was drunk, why, everybody knows about his drinking problem. Zumwalt will fire him for that speech and then he won't be wobbling about so high and mighty." Flinch drank some whiskey from a wax cup he'd brought out of the bar. He slipped on some ice, went up into the air, and came down crashing on a hip. There was a sharp pain in his side. A car pulled up. Blitz was in the front seat. He was with three little men who worked with Big North's boiling, churning chocolate vats. Blitz helped him into the car. "Boy, Blitz," Savvage said, "am I glad to see you." Blitz didn't say anything.

28

Saturday's generation believed in Santa Claus until they were at least twenty-one. Some left out soup and cookies for him until they were twenty-six or even forty. When they found out that there was no Santa Claus, no unlimited filled stockings hanging from the fireplace, they began to haunt the bars west of Fifth Avenue and vowed never to go above Fourteenth Street again. They were nurtured on novels in which the protagonist expressed little emotion upon receiving news that his mother had died.

During the epidemic of child murders the Atlanta Public Safety Commissioner described his methodology in the following manner. When you come to a brick wall, you either tear down the wall or start in a new direction. Apparently, he tore down the wall and solved the case. For Nance, that approach lacked elegance. He approached a problem as a romantic would. He would read material. He would study all the trivia connected with the case and all the facts he could sew together and usually the solution would come. If that didn't work, then he'd have to try the other method. Tear down the wall, or, in this case, open the door.

Saturday was lying in bed, reading about the historical Saint Nicholas as well as the legend, Nicholas. He spent the day in the library on 42nd Street. Books lay on one side of him. Articles and clippings on the other side. Sometimes he had to literally climb into bed with the facts before he could come up with something. A white plate holding a peanut butter sandwich lay on his stomach. He drank from a glass of acidophilus milk and examined photos from different books. He recognized the picture of the Boy Bishop, one of the darlings of New York Society, posing with some women at a dog show. In another, he was attending an auction of antiques. There was the Boy Bishop whom Jamaica Queens talked of, surrounded by his followers, all similarly dressed in black priest's clothes.

The church was always nervous that Nicholas's reputation would outflank Christ's. Not only had he performed miracles and raised the dead as Christ had done, not only was he ubiquitous as Christ was, but he could fly as well. Christ could ascend, but Nicholas could fly! The Vatican, as the years passed, became more and more hostile to Nicholas. In 1969, the Pope declared Nicholas "moribund."

Saturday could understand why Nicholas also offended the Puritans so much that they banned his holiday. There was an illustration of Nicholas, the jolly old man, with a laurel wreath on his head and a silver cup full of wine, naked from the waist up, surrounded by half-clad women, presiding over a decadent and voluptuous supper. His waist was a pink Goodyear tire. Oral sex was suggested. And about the dolls: the dolls symbolized a rite of a much earlier Christmas which had to do with infanticide. The dreadful Winter Solstice. The days are shorter and the undead, the half dead, and the near dead roam the world, have a chance to stay out a bit longer to haunt the living. Here was one. An illustration of Saint Nicholas, but peeking from behind him is a coxcombed black figure with a bunch of rods sticking out of a pouch he carries on his back. *Black Peter!* Jamaica Queens told him something about a rivalry between Boy Bishop and "Peter." He is described as a Moor. Later, he is a Spanish figure. He was among those who came to the Netherlands during the Spanish occupation under Philip II, whom one historian accused of having "degenerate blood." Somebody suggests that Black Peter symbolizes the Dutch's hatred of the Spanish.

St. Nicholas rides a white horse (Odin?) and Black Peter follows behind, carrying a sack, and wearing page-boy clothes: plumed hat, black doublet, hose, and black gloves. And just as you'd expect, it was Black Peter's job to go down the chimney.

From the Tretyakov Gallery in Moscow, a devil escaping from a man's mouth. A tiny black creature with long body and a big nose and a rooster's crown. Saint Nicholas was exorcising the man. Just like the Dutch. Instead of dissolving the devil, Saint Nicholas makes him carry his bags. Or is it Peter who makes Nicholas carry his bag? A close reading of the legend leads one to question who is the master of whom, and sometimes Nicholas and Peter are interchangeable! Black Peter drops from the Santa Claus (Nicholas) legend because, according to an issue of the *Knickerbocker Weekly*, Santa couldn't find hotel reservations for his servant, or master, if you will, "due to American racial customs."

The Americans would soon find out what the Dutch, French, and English had learned before. It's hard to prevent Black Peter from going where he wants to go.

It was 2:00 A.M. Clear-thinking time. The noise of the day had abated. The gloaming had been blood red. Christmas sounded more like Halloween. The night of the Kallikaritori. Dreadful and allusive shapes which caused mischief. The Evil One. Zombies trundled. Body snatching. All of the body snatching connected to the Nicholas legend. The Saint's remains had been moved from Kiev, to Bari, to New York.

The newspaper clippings showed the Boy Bishop, TV-blond hair, goatee, impeccably dressed. His followers begged in the airports while he made the Long Island scene standing next to one of Capote's subjects, or he could be seen blessing a society wedding party.

The Nicholas people were organized. They were rumored to have a cruel way of dealing with their enemies. Once a neighbor complained about them and was sent a box of tarantulas. They bugged people and broke into their homes for incriminating evidence. One of their techniques was out-and-out extortion. They stuck together. When there were public meetings against them they sometimes showed up in full force. On this, Saturday went to sleep at the kitchen table, a light still on.

29

Early in the afternoon, a hand reached out from behind the door of Nicholas House and brought in the leaflet. Someone was calling for a neighborhood meeting to discuss the deteriorating situation at Nicholas House which threatened the safety of the neighborhood. There was an address on the leaflet, which also promised coffee, cake, and child care. Sure enough, at about 8:00 P.M., the people streamed out of the house into their BMW's and headed for the address on the leaflet, about thirty blocks across town.

Saturday figured it would take them about a half hour to reach the house whose address appeared on the leaflet, ten minutes to discover that they'd been tricked, and a half hour to return, which would give him time to search the place. As soon as the last black sedan of hooded people turned the corner, he headed across the street towards the Nicholas house clutching his cap against the strong ocean winds. This was what he'd been waiting many days for. An event that would get everybody out of the house. When he reached the door he started jimmying the locks.

30

His research having failed to turn up a clue about Snow Man, Saturday decided to take the bull by the horns. You would have thought that Saturday was a hummingbird, the way he whirred about the Nicholas house, taking notes and flashing pictures. Pictures of furnishings, paintings, altars, of different rooms. He found the office and went to work on the files. "Nicholas." "Winter Solstice." "Boy Bishop." "Financial Statements." "Check Stubs." "I.R.S. Non-Profit." "Donors."

"Real Estate." They owned choice properties on Long Island, Staten Island, Brooklyn, and Manhattan. They owned a retreat in the Massachusetts woods. "Nicholas," someone had written, "the most popular Saint in Russia" in longhand. Not only was Nicholas connected with body snatching, but some-one had included, in this file, an old story about Nicholas.

About how all the Saints were seated about, getting drunk on Saint wine, when one noticed that Nicholas was dozing. When asked why, he said that though his body was there dozing his spirit was at sea, rescuing sailors. In a curious scrawl, there was a note tracing Russia's problems to a debate between Saint Nicholas and Saint Elijah. "Donors": this file included some of the illustrious names of the New York social, political, and cultural world. "Zumwalt." There was a photo of a young man who resembled Oswald Zumwalt. He wore a t-shirt with the name "Harvard" written on it. He was standing next to a very pretty young girl. She wore pigtails, a baggy sweater and pleated skirt. She was a short brunette. He had his arm about her. Though the chin had dropped and the nose was a little larger, it was Zumwalt. There was an old clipping from a New York newspaper about the death of the son of model, Dean Clift, at Harvard. "Suspect sought." There was a Xerox of an invoice from a Beverly Hills plastic surgeon. He continued his search through the files. "Roman Catholic Church." There was a story about a Vatican investigator who was fished out of the East River. He was identified as a member of the Holy Office. Someone had underlined *Holy Office* and in the margin had written "Inquisition." Saturday found nothing about Snow Man. He had to leave. They'd be returning soon.

He grabbed a bunch of papers and stuffed them into his briefcase. It was then that he heard someone calling for help. The sound was coming from the basement. It was a pitiful desperate cry. It belonged to a man. Snow Man? He was about to head into the basement when he heard the sound of the first BMW returning. Saturday ran from the room and climbed through a window. He made it before the first key turned in the lock. He jumped into his black Ford and drove off. He hoped that he would have something to report to Joe Baby the next day.

31

They may have behaved like tough punks, but they were, after all, schoolboys, and so when they heard that an anonymous hotel guest had ordered cream fudge, sodas, sundaes with bananas, cherries, and topped with pistachio nuts for them, they dropped their maces, hammers, pop guns, brass knuckles, baseball bats, and bricks, abandoned their vigil at Santa's suite, and flew into the elevator, knocking one another over. Peeking from behind the corner, Vixen, seeing that the coast was clear, tiptoed towards Santa's suite. She opened the door with a key given to her by the bell captain. She had told him that she wanted to surprise Santa, as she pressed cash into his hand. She marveled at the decorations of the suite which were done in an old Spanish style. There was lots of red: red drapes, red carpets, red wallpaper. She heard some muttering coming from behind the curtains, which formed the entrance to the suite's main room. She drew them aside. There was a little black man, standing on a stool, holding a milk bottle between Santa's lips. Santa was lying in a raspberry-red casket. The little man's head swung about with not so much as a turn from his torso, like the girl's in *The Exorcist*—before blacking out, Vixen was struck by her ability to be able to see his face and heels at the same time. He looked like one of those cute little colored boy tap dancers with them bright smiles and them shiny eyes and shoes. Santa's eyes blinked and then sinisterly darted in her direction. She began to babble as she slowly sank to the carpet, and when they found her across town, in a vacant lot, stuffed in what appeared to be a mail bag, nearly frozen, she was still babbling, until she stopped babbling and was unable to make any sound.

32

Crossroads figures in Vodoun are associated with elevators because going from time to time is like riding in an elevator. The time elevator is such a smooth ride that you feel as if you're standing still. Nicholas and Dean Clift didn't know when the elevator they had taken from the third world to the tenth world had stopped. They exited and walked towards what appeared to be a medieval fortress with the heads of turrets showing above the ledges of the walls. The turrets resembled shark fins. There was so much fog that it was hard to tell what the purpose of this building was. Soon they found out. Behind the walls lay a prison which was shaped like a square with its sides labeled Block A, Block B, Block C, and Block D. The sides were connected by four tunnels which enclosed Yard A, Yard B, Yard C, and Yard D. Standing before Block A was an administration building, a place haunted with urgent whispers, just as they occurred on the day of the tragedy. Ghost helicopters could be seen hovering above the yards.

Where the tunnels connect there is a place called Times Square and while, on that day, many hostages were there, now there was only one.

The President and the Saint stopped, right outside the prison wall, and the permanent ghostly procession began. First, the smiling Gussucks, wearing blue helmets and gray coveralls with huge pockets. They were carrying the shotguns. Strapped to the coveralls were green gas masks. They wore combat boots. The four men in the lead were grinning into the cameras of a popular news weekly magazine. Next, a blond surgeon, wearing black rubber boots with yellow toes and a green surgeon's gown, covered with blood. He and the reporters, hanging on his every word, scribbling in their notebooks, passed by the President and the Saint. The President started to speak as the group disappeared into the fog.

Suddenly, a group of figures shuffled rapidly towards them. They seemed to be doing some kind of jazz step. They were in prison clothes and were armed with broom handles and sticks. He recognized the man chained to them, even though the man wore a blindfold. He was richly dressed in silk pajamas, a housecoat with his monogram on it, and expensive leather slippers. The others were masked. They wore ski masks and stockings over their heads. A glimpse of a nose bridge here and some dark skin there suggested to the President that some were Negroes. The color of an eye here and nose-shape there meant that the rest were white. Some wore prisoner's uniforms, others were wearing the uniforms of guards. But if you glanced at their feet, you saw coyote's paws. In death, the Governor's grin had become sardonic. He had purple lips and a yellow face. His hair was wild and blue. It never occurred to the President when he knew this man in life how much he resembled the Joker in the Batman comics. The President and the Saint looked upon the man with pity.

"I know what you're thinking," the blue-haired one said. "I died with my pants down. My rump showing. And my dick out. So you're the new President. Heady wine, being President. I wanted that job. I wanted it with every sinew and enzyme of my body. I thought these men gave me the opportunity. My party thought that I was too easy with blacks. My party taunted me about the welfare programs in my state. They told me that if I could bring some nigger's balls to roast they'd let me have what I wanted. And so when these prisoners revolted at one of my jails, I sent the troopers in. Members of my party in Arizona, Texas, and Utah phoned me their congratulations. Dick called from the White House. I was feeling good. This gave me more thrills than my art collection, my horses, and my homes. I loved this glory more than I loved my children. It made me hard. I started to rise like the flag over Iwo Jima. Henry was right, power is an aphrodisiac. I felt the testes shoring up within. I felt like I could squirt it from here to across the continent. I called my friend and told her to meet me. I loved that woman. Southern girl. She used to call me her old billy goat. She'd give me golden showers and other techniques she was so good at. And then she would scold me. I mean really scold me, no hedging or pussy-footing around. She'd tell me that I was a real jerkball regardless of my money and my original Seurats and Matisses. She brought a girl with her. She had the other girl's tongue in her ass and I was on top of her, and the little tart called me corny and started spanking me on the butt. The phone rang. I let it ring. I was having a good time. I was feeling no pain. And so when the phone kept ringing I took out the plug. The next morning they told me. They said they'd been trying to reach me all night. The fuckers had gone into the jail and killed over thirty people. The fuckers were only supposed to kill a few to show those people in the Southwest how tough I was. How I wasn't just a stupid rich boy with café society connections, but how I could really get the job done. Do you know what else? They killed white men. They killed the hostages. I guess I was nothing but a polo bum after all; a gelding. All the fathers I killed. And so I have to go about chained to my crimes.

"I have to go and watch their kids and their grandkids and their great-grandkids. Watch them as they ask what happened to their fathers. Watch the orphans under the Christmas trees. Watch the little tots walk home alone. I have to watch the crying mothers, daughters, sisters. I wasn't an evil man. Just thoughtless. As these men say, I never paid no dues. I could have been a great man. That meant something then, but it doesn't mean anything now. Watch what you're doing, Mr. President. If you just pay attention and don't get excited, you'll do the right thing. Then you won't have to go through what Harry had to go through. Dreams tailing you. You won't end up like me. Chained to my crimes. Death shouldn't be like this. Do you know what Death is? It's like you've been running all day and you've had a great day, and your heart is thumping real hard, and you lie down under a birch tree, near a cool river like the Connecticut River, and the soft wind is faintly caressing your cheeks, lifting a few strands of hair, and you just rest, and somebody offers you a cold beer. Death is like a cold beer you get after you've been running too hard. Golden slumbers. The song Sarah sang for Errol Garner. It shouldn't be like this. It shouldn't be like this. This, this has no logic."

The other men pulled him away and soon they were shuffling backwards into darkness. Even Saint Nicholas had to shake his head. The President was sobbing, as the Governor faded with his strange escorts into the fog, trying to manage a chipper smile. He turned a final time and called, "Let what happened to me and to Harry be a lesson to you, Mr. President. Always follow love, beauty, and truth, and you can't go wrong. Do good deeds and help the poor, the downtrodden, and the sick—I know that sounds sentimental in the cutthroat world above, but those things mean a hell of a lot down here. And whatever you do, never listen to your generals, the way Harry did, or trust those super sleuths who creep about the halls of buildings with no windows. Ike's mistake. Be sure that your Secretary of State has a sense of humor and doesn't have any women preachers in his family. If you see somebody coming towards you wearing a homburg, turn and walk in the other direction; and, Mr. President, whatever you do, don't trust your scientists. If there is such a thing as hell on earth, you can be sure they'll get around to unleashing it one of these days."

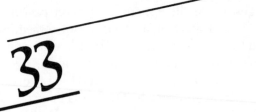

The incredible Christmas events had gotten Jack Frost to thinking. Jack Frost wasn't a thoughtful man; he had a lizard's brain and a vicious cunning which was trained to sense the heart of an intended victim. In his former career, Jack had left the second-story men, the petty scams and the mugging, in favor of the cat-burglar profession. He was always dressed as dapperly as Fred Astaire and sometimes would imitate Astaire's bouncy, cootie walk. But things at Big North had turned around so he had the distinct impression that the world was moving counterclockwise. Why had the relationship between Santa and Zumwalt changed? Why was Santa, who was always Zumwalt's victim, now calling the shots for Big North? And the taunts of the black bellhop.

The story was all over the newspapers. The business pages doubted that a successful Christmas could be had after Santa's incendiary speech. Department store inventories were stalled after Santa's admonition to his followers to boycott the big bosses. Some even suggested that it was all a trick by Zumwalt to corner the Christmas season and Santa Claus too. The scheme, according to these financial observers, was to steer all the business to the domed city Zumwalt was building on the North Pole. But others discounted this theory, claiming that by sabotaging the Christmas of 1990, Zumwalt was going to make it hard to get his bill through Congress. Most agreed that Zumwalt had a great deal to lose by having Santa call for a boycott against his clients. To add to Zumwalt's problem, a shipment of candy from Big North had arrived containing human hair, bones, and bits of nails. The Food and Drug Administration was investigating. And what puzzled Jack Frost more than anything was Zumwalt's silence. He remained locked in a suite that formerly belonged to Santa. Why had he given Santa his expensive suite? Jack Frost was faithful to Oswald Zumwalt. Zumwalt had stood by him during the trial. Frost had been charged with murdering his grandmother when she caught him stealing her jewels. The state didn't have enough to convict. Besides, Jack's grandmother, a snow-haired, crooked-nosed woman with black high-button shoes, was a bigger thief than Jack. Jack's men, the Floorwalkers, Big North's security guards, were scattered throughout their suite. Some were cleaning their pistols, others were playing cards, or listening to the radio or watching television. Others were in the kitchen preparing spaghetti. Still others were drinking beer. Suddenly one of their men burst into the room. He was accompanied by a lean, shivering man who looked like Howard Hughes in his last days. The aide had wrapped a blanket around him. Jack Frost sprang to his feet, and his men stopped doing what they were doing and gazed at the scene.

"What's this all about?" said Jack.

"He says he's the real Santa Claus and that the man upstairs is an imposter."

"How do you know he's not lying?" Frost asked the Floorwalker who had brought in the man who claimed to be Santa Claus.

"I know he's not lying. Go on, say it," the man said to Santa.

"Ho. Ho. Ho."

"That's him all right," Jack said. He'd recognize Rex Stuart's Ho. Ho. Ho. anywhere.

"Where are they now?" Jack Frost said, preparing his gunbelt. The other Floorwalkers did likewise.

"They've left for the Garden. For the annual Christmas Feast and Variety Show."

Jack Frost led the men to Madison Square Garden.

34

St. Nicholas and the President stood in an expensive though messy hotel room located about two blocks from the White House. It could have been a suite in the Sheraton. St. Nicholas beckoned the President to follow him into the bedroom. There was a mahogany console which was playing one of Beethoven's last quartets. The room was disheveled. Standing next to the window was a distinguished-looking, gray-haired man. He held a glass of rare Bordeaux in his hand. He was staring out the window. He seemed nervous and he was smoking cigarettes one after another. He could hear some guests arguing about money in the next room. The traffic was loud outside. On the bedroom wall was a Remington the President had given to his Secretary of Defense. That's who it was, his Secretary of Defense. He called him by name. St. Nicholas told him that the Secretary of Defense couldn't hear him and that the only reason the rich Governor could hear him was because the rich and powerful communicate even in hell and that the devil's cabinet has some of the most illustrious names of world history; that's why God isn't rid of the devil, because God gets his advice from mostly dull minds. The Secretary of Defense was admired by the nation because of his integrity and his honesty. He was a man who loved life. Into water sports and jogging and racquetball, but he'd also written some poetry and played the piano. But the Secretary of Defense had been accused of not realizing the threat this peculiar and dangerous foreign nation posed to the security of the free world and Western values.

The Secretary of Defense had opposed the military establishment and spoken out against the Congressmen and Pentagon officials who were always trying to burden the taxpayers with outdated carriers and obsolete bombers. Just as he was about to deliver a major speech before the National Press Club, in which he was to speak harshly against the secret plan of the Colorado Gang, code name Two Birds, and leak it to the press, he leaped from the window of a Washington hotel. They had to hose down his remains.

Nicholas and the model President watched the Secretary of Defense gaze from a window towards the White House, which stood in the distance. He began to talk to himself. "The President, poor dope, doesn't know the half of it, as long as he indulges himself with his ten tailors, his hat designers, and his custom shoe makers—as long as he makes the glittering rounds of Washington society, he's happy, and he really, if he wanted to, could change the course of—there I go again. My idealism. He should hear how they refer to him as the model and how they sneer at him at their private parties. All those years. Splashing that language about like bad vodka in a Bloody Mary. Kill ratios. Cruise missiles. MERV. MC. SST. Stealth. Invisible bombers. Space satellites. Laser beams. The whole bloody carapace with which the nations cover themselves. But now with this Two Bird plan, they've really blown the coop.

"Mean-spirited idiots. They're going to get us all blown up. If this country knew what mindless, ignorant, selfish men rule, they'd rise up and hang them by their silk Japanese underwear. O, what's coming over me? I just do what I have to do. I must warn the country of what the King of Beer, Bob Krantz, Reverend Jones, and Admiral Matthews are about to concoct. I must stop them before the missiles come raining down on New York and Miami. And then their plan is to blame the attacks on a hostile foreign power, thereby providing rationale for devastating that power, and the surplus people and the UDC's too. Operation Two Birds! A plan to take care of the enemy and the surplus people at the same time."

The President's lower jaw dropped. He stiffened. He turned to St. Nicholas, who merely nodded his head and smiled, faintly. The Secretary of Defense left the window and sat at his desk. The FM radio was now playing Brahms' Fourth Symphony. He took a sip of wine. He began to read from the speech that would blow the whistle on Reverend Jones and his cohorts.

"John F. Kennedy, when he fought big steel, spoke of selfish men who use their power to cause hard times for the American people. He, in his wildest dreams, did not know how selfish they were. The common citizen could never imagine how selfish they were. So selfish that they would destroy the world if it got in the way of their profits, then write the world off as a tax deduction.

"What do you think those space ships are for, you fools? So that the executives of multinational corporations and their company men and servants will be able to sit out the holocaust on another planet. Sit it out in luxury, maybe on Mars where the temperatures in some places are like those of San Francisco. All they know is consume and produce, consume and produce like a tapeworm which spends its life evacuating and copulating with itself and like the tapeworm they don't pay their way.

"We know they don't care about their fellow citizens. In the fifties and sixties germ warfare was practiced on unsuspecting citizens in New York and San Francisco. And now, their most heinous plan is about to come to fruition. These power-crazed men are preparing to unleash the most awful weapon of all. They plan to drop a bomb on— Maybe I should tone it down a bit—but then, who will understand it? No. I'll speak my mind. The issues are too important to gloss over with glib platitudes. But, then, maybe they'll dismiss me as a bitter malcontent if I don't tone it down." The buzzer rang. The Secretary of Defense rose to answer the doorbell. Two burly Gussucks with crewcuts and blank foreheads forced their way in. They owned the dumb, idiotic stares of sharks. The fragile and bookish Secretary of Defense struggled, but it was impossible for him to overwhelm these men who maneuvered him over to the window after knocking over chairs and tables. One man choked the Secretary of Defense as he forced him out of the window, but the Secretary of Defense put up a struggle. The President tried to rush to his cabinet officer's defense, but he was paralyzed. He turned to St. Nicholas, but Nicholas had disappeared. The scene went black as he kept yelling the Secretary of Defense's name: "Andrew, Andrew, Annnnn-drewwwwwww."

"Wake up, Mr. President."

"Huh." The President looked towards the window. He rubbed his eyes.

"Where's the coffin? Where's my wife?"

"We buried her three days ago, Mr. President. Don't you remember? When we got back you came into this room. You said you wanted to be left alone."

"O, yes. Yes, I remember." The President looked out of the window. The snow was blazing white and sparkling from the sun. The cold wind delightfully nipped at cheeks and ears. It was a bright, beautiful Washington day. "John, get me a cup of coffee and the *Post*, will you?"

"Yessir, Mr. President."

"And by the way," the President said, yawning.

"What's that, Mr. President?" John said, turning to the Chief Executive.

"What day is it?"

"It's December twenty-fifth. Christmas Day, sir."

"Merry Christmas, John," the President said with a rare smile.

"Merry Christmas to you, Mr. President," John said.

35

Big Meat answered the door. Saturday stood there, glum. He could tell that Big Meat had been sobbing. Big Meat led him into the apartment that Joe Baby and he shared. There was a sweet, acrid odor in the air. Silk was used extensively in the furnishings, the bedspeads and the chair covers, the pillows. The curtains were laced and dainty. There were frills and bows all over the place. There was some "African" sculpture throughout the room. *Ebony* magazine lay on the coffee table.

"Where's Joe Baby?"

"Joe Baby is dead," Big Meat said, and began to hold his head in his hands and sob some more.

"Dead, how did that happen?" Saturday said, going to the liquor cabinet and pouring himself a brandy and branch water.

"It happened last night. Christmas Eve. We were sitting in the bar and this punk began to hassle Joe Baby. Teased him about the Boy Bishop who took his women, and the Snow Man who ran off with his money.

"He got into a shouting match with the punk; the other players had been respectful to Joe Baby but there was a silly boy from Memphis. He didn't know Joe Baby's reputation. He didn't know that Joe Baby was a man of distinction." Big Meat went through an episode of sobbing. "The punk kept goading him and even when some of the other players tried to restrain the punk out of respect for Joe Baby, the punk kept going and then the punk invited Joe Baby outside, and I leaped between Joe Baby and the punk. I was going to flash the punk but Joe Baby said he fought his own fights.

"The country spook started out in front of Joe Baby, and Joe Baby whacked him across the head, lifted him by the hind seat and tossed him outside. Everybody was laughing. Joe Baby began to laugh and then he grimaced and grabbed at his chest. His eyes went kinda white and he fell to the floor, knocking some glasses off the bar, and he began convulsing and twitching. I tried to give him mouth to mouth. But—" Big Meat clutched his hotcomb-straightened hair, his wrists revealing huge, glitzy bracelets, his hands sparkling with rings. He was wearing a pink Frenchified shirt, pink pants, and white shoes. He looked like a flamingo. "We managed to get him to the hospital. He lived for a few hours."

"I really tried to find Snow Man. I went through everything. I interviewed a journalist who had written an article about Boy Bishop's people; I staked out their mansion and found no sign of Snow Man or Boy Bishop; I even broke into the place trying to find evidence. O, well, eventually it will come. It's too bad. I really need the cash."

"That reminds me," Big Meat said. "Joe Baby told me to give you this envelope. He said to enjoy. I figured that the Boy Bishop and the Snow Man struck some kind of deal and split off with the money. Who knows?"

"There's no evidence of that. Just a bunch of strung-out kids, if you ask me, those Nicolaites. There's even a blood mixed up with them."

"These black kids today. They're really attracted to that offbeat stuff. Reggae. Dreadlocks. Strange philosophies." Nance Saturday had opened the envelope to find a lot of cash.

"What's this for?"

"He wanted you to have it. He told me in the hospital. He said that you were right about him not using his ability to the fullest. He said he should have done something more worthwhile with his life. Those last few hours. He seemed to be really at peace. The nurse told me that an old man dressed in priestly clothes was talking to him after I left. It must have been the hospital chaplain administering last rites."

"Well, in that case, I think I'll keep the money. I did put a lot of time into the case. It was an interesting assignment. Educational. Where's the bathroom?"

Big Meat pointed, and grinned, revealing a gold upper tooth. Nance Saturday went into the bathroom. He walked on a round rug the color of pink sherbet, and used the toilet. There were posters on the wall of Montgomery Clift dressed as Sigmund Freud, and Marlon Brando in black leather and cap, seated on a motorcycle. He washed his hands with the pink Camay soap. He walked out into the living room and put on his wolfskin parka and snowshoes.

"Man, you dressed up like you're fixing to drive a dogsled."

"I'm warm," Nance said. "What are you going to do now that Joe Baby is dead?"

"I'm getting out of this street shit and going into a new profession—a profession where I don't have to worry about cops bothering me."

"What kind of profession is that?"

"White collar crime." Nance looked at the black strands of processed hair and flecks of dirt on Big Meat's collar, and burst out laughing.

"Did I say something funny?" Big Meat asked.

36

My grandfather works at the White House. He's been there for thirty years. I don't have anybody to live with me because my folks died in an automobile accident. I was there when it happened, and my leg hurt for months after the accident. They had to take my leg off. Me and my grandfather live together in Washington and as soon as I feel better I'm going back to school. I love school. In school we read a lot of books. My grandfather reads a lot of books, too. He reads Booker T. Washington, J. A. Rogers, W.E.B. DuBois, James Weldon Johnson, Marcus Garvey. He knows a lot about the personal lives of the Presidents he's worked for.

While I was in the hospital, my grandfather brought me lots of magazines. *Newsweek, Time, Ebony, U.S. News and World Report, Africa, Jet,* and the *Amsterdam News.* I love to read about history and current events. Well, let me tell you this Christmas morning I got the current events surprise of my life. My grandfather had to work at the White House. Esther and Joan, who work at the White House with my grandfather, were cooking our Christmas dinner and I was playing with this swell pigskin basketball my grandfather bought me for Christmas. I'm crazy about basketball and I have pictures of Wilt Chamberlain and Bill Russell on the wall of my room. Well, I was playing with my basketball and having a good time when we heard my grandfather's key turn in the lock. We were waiting for my grandfather to enter when we heard two voices behind the door. Was grandfather bringing another guest to dinner? When the door opened, we could see that it was my grandfather and his boss, the President of the United States, his arms full of gifts tied with different-colored ribbons. I recognized him from his pictures. Esther and Joan didn't seem so glad to see him. I've heard them say bad things about the President and his wife. But my grandfather shuts them up. He tells them that they ought to have respect for the President since, after all, he is the nation's leader. He is the leader of the blacks and the whites, and the rich and the poor, and if he is rude to the White House staff it's because he has a lot of things on his mind. My grandfather says that if the President pushes a little button all of us will go the way of the dinosaur, although I've read that there are still dinosaurs hanging around the Congo River. Little dinosaurs. My grandfather asked the women to fix an extra plate for the President, and after a bit of grumbling they did what he asked. We sat down to eat and my grandfather asked the President would he like to have a drink before the meal, and the President says that he thinks he'll pass because he has some big decisions to make and that he wants to have a clear head since some of these decisions may affect the course of the human history or something like that. The food was terrific. We had chicken, mashed potatoes with gravy, peas and corn, biscuits, and potato pie, which is my favorite. The President said that he had a son like me who was killed when he fell on a fence, and that for years he carried a grudge against the kid responsible even though it sounded as if it was an accident. He said he was going to call off the search for the man who wounded his son. He said he was going to devote his time to healing the nation's wounds. He says he's going to send me to a hospital named Walter Reed to see if there's something that his own personal physician could do for me.

The President said that there were some bad men in the Pentagon and the Foreign Service who were on the payroll of men who make airplanes and bombs and that these men didn't care when Russia, China, and India got the H-Bomb, but when Nigeria got one, these men called him all day and night asking what he was going to do with these black niggers who had the H-Bomb. He said that they had tried to convince him that if all of black Africa got H-Bombs, they would fling them about every Saturday night after they got drunk on palm wine. He said that these bad, sick men had proposed that they drop a bomb on New York and pretend that the Nigerians did it, and then they'd have an excuse to wipe out Nigeria, and New York at the same time. I figured that these men had something against New York. He said that he was going to go on television and tell the nation about something called Operation Two Birds. He said that when he died he didn't want to be followed by some nagging bad dream, nor did he want to wander about for an eternity chained to his crimes. Well, we all looked at one another. I thought that I was the only one who didn't understand what the President was saying, but Joan and Esther tried to suppress a sniggle; only my grandfather played like nothing strange was said. I guess he hears the President talk this way all the time. The President has a lot of things on his mind since his wife was killed. The President talked about how he was playing footsies with the Nazis because he had to carry some states in the Midwest and California. He started sobbing and asking my grandfather's forgiveness. He said it was the biggest mistake he ever made and that he hoped he hadn't offended the colored people and the Jews. He said that he loved the Jews. That he loved their great sense of humor and was crazy about their food. And when he goes to New York he always makes it his business to visit Leo Steiner's Carnegie Deli for his delicious bagels and cream cheese. He said that this man named Adolf Hitler was a monster and that it was a shame that the Congress of the United States would set aside a holiday for Adolf Hitler and still hadn't done anything about Martin Luther King, Jr., who had more integrity in his fingernail than a hundred Franklin Roosevelts. He said that within the last twenty-four hours God had sent him a revelation and that now he knew what he must do. He said that he knew how colored people had been spat on for so many years. He said that the whole world admired the way black people kept on keeping on, surrounded by a hostile nation of dumb son-of-a-bitch squatters. He said that the squatters of America were crazy and that Santa Claus had a point when he said they were acting like emotional two-year-olds. Wanting to have twenty-five-inch-screen color TV sets in every room. Winnebagos, microwave ovens. He said it's time that the United States, which uses forty-five percent of the world's resources, changed its own diapers. He apologized to me and the women but said he'd never been really mad and that it was a new experience for him.

He told Esther, Joan, and my grandfather that he'd set the whole thing right. He said that he was going to give them all raises. Well, when he said that, Esther and Joan grinned for the first time since the President came into the house. He said that he was going to invite Marion Brown to play at the White House and he said that he was going to do this and do that and then the President got up and put on his coat. He said he was going to go to the White House and call up the President of Nigeria to go in with him to call an international conference to get rid of everything from nuclear weapons and missiles down to hand guns and pocket knives, tweezers, and can openers. He said there was nothing wrong with the twist. He said that the billions of dollars devoted to weaponry could go into making the world a paradise since man had at least a few more billion years before the universe blew up. He said that man's life should be filled with artful and spiritual things. He came over to me and pressed a hundred-dollar bill and a season's pass to the Washington Redskins' games in my hand. He then gathered the gifts and placed them under our Christmas tree. We heard him outside, walking down the stairs singing "Jingle

Bells." My grandfather came back and sat down at the table. He just kept shaking his head and mumbling something about how he'll never be able to figure white folks out.

The President stood outside the tenement building. He stretched and felt the crisp, morning air on his face. Once inside his limousine, he directed the driver to return to the White House, but changed his mind. "Driver, take me to the Holiday Inn on Rhode Island, I think it is. I'll move in there temporarily. I don't want to return to that house, a house of slaveholders, Indian killers, apartheid advocates, crypto-Klu Kluxers, and other eminent landlord types. What's this country doing with an executive mansion that's copycat French anyway? And that Beaux Arts eyesore across the street, I'd like to get rid of that too. The same guy who designed Grant's Tomb must have designed this town with its statues of Latin American dictators on horseback, all pointing at nothing. I'd like a White House that, that's a little more indigenous."

Before the car pulled away, the President glanced up at one of the windows of the apartment he'd just left. John's grandson stood in the window waving. The President waved back. The snow was beginning to melt and soon there would be the smell of Japanese cherry blossoms in the air. The President leaned back in the seat, his hands supporting his head.

"Driver."

"Yes, Mr. President."

"You take the rest of the day off. On Christmas, men should be with their families. You tell the Secret Service, too."

The driver smiled. "Yessir, Mr. President."

"Also, get Air Force One ready for a trip to that sanitorium where they have my daughter. I'm going to spend the rest of the holidays with her."

37

Zumwalt was seated in Santa's room, wearing a maroon bathrobe, blue silk pajamas, and deerskin slippers. He was listening to some gloomy imperialistic music. The kind that used to be used at the official dedication of mausoleums. Sir William Walton.

Ten years had passed since he had had his boss for Thanksgiving dinner. A turkey like the one they had that day would cost seventy-five dollars today. He thought of his break-up with his wife, Jane, his rapid rise in the Schneider Department Store, Herman Schneider's dismissal by the Texans, and George Schneider's death. He had received a Christmas card from a nursing home with Herman's strained, weak signature on it. He never answered. He had sent a confidential report to the Texans on the money-wasting practices of the Schneider brothers. Based upon this report, the brothers had been dismissed by the Texans and Zumwalt was hired to replace them as the store's president. As long as Zumwalt kept the profits coming in, his bosses in Texas never complained.

With the contacts his new job brought he was able to accumulate the wealth necessary to launch his dream to obtain the exclusive rights to Santa Claus; whoever controlled Santa Claus, controlled Christmas. And so now, Big North had hundreds of employees and after the domed city was completed he would have hundreds more. The Christmas season produced a hundred times more profit than the World Series, Mardi Gras, and the Superbowl combined. The domed city at the North Pole would outgross all the Disneylands. And Jane? From time to time he would think of her, the close-cropped brunette hair, her chubby face, her causes, and the way she used to squirm and squeal with delight under him. She was one of the few women of her generation content with the missionary position.

He had known that sooner or later his past's awful secret would catch up with him, and now it had. Sir William's depressing, brooding strings from a "Falstaff" theme engulfed the room. Zumwalt reached for some more pills.

What had gone wrong? He remembered when he got up in Mississippi to begin another day of black voter registration. And then the Indians, and the women, and the Mexicans, and the boat people, and on and on until he got sick of it. A lot of his white male friends felt the same way. And then 1981, and the reign of Rawhide began. He said what they all felt. He didn't even have to say it. The way he shrugged his shoulders, and innocently spread his hands before the cameras as if to say, "Who, me?" There was something in his every gesture which said "Who the hell is worrying about the white man?" Who *was* looking out for the white men in England, Australia, South Africa, West Germany, and the rest of the free world? White men were fucking bleeding themselves to death over seals and the handicapped, but who was looking out for them, buddy? I mean, when you think about it, they were the ones who were oppressed, outnumbered by women and "minorities" who were getting everything. Nobody but Rawhide gave a shit about them.

They were oppressed by having to look after everybody else. Kipling was right. And so Rawhide, though not all that popular among women and minorities, always polled in the high sixties among white men. He was telling them, fuck affirmative action, this sambo or this whore is trying to take your fucking job, Charlie, and you'd better get wise to it, pal. And so the early and middle eighties were grand times for white men as the country halted its "social experiments," eschewed the "secular humanist philosophy," and hit the beaches, running.

Oswald Zumwalt had reached the American Olympus during that period and found that there the only people you saw were Caucasian males. O, maybe a Japanese here and there. Zumwalt was beginning to miss his black friends. At least they got excited from time to time. At least they knew how to blow their tops. The white men at the top never got excited, and when they did they could always zip off in their private planes or get some Feelgood Park Avenue doctor to give them a legal high. People didn't fall in love at the top. Love was something like a refreshment, or a dry martini, or a nice hot bath.

Nobody came to visit him anymore. His old friends. He wondered what had happened to them. Some had begun farms in Maine and Vermont. He saw the fleeting images of others as they were dragged from anti-nuclear demonstrations. Some of them still cared about the poor. The poor. He almost threw up as he and the Mayor had ridden from the barge to Gracie Mansion. It wasn't just Mayor Grouch's conversation—all about the Mayor—but the sight of the sore-ridden, emaciated arms reaching out to touch him, or the abject, demoralized eyes which stared at him, and the screams the Mayor didn't acknowledge that came from the roving desperate as the police whipped them to keep them out of view of the cameras which were broadcasting to the nation Santa's arrival into Manhattan. And now, Santa acts up. What had come over Santa? So meek that he seldom said more than a few sentences. The stirring speech he'd made at Times Square. He would never have thought that Rex Stuart, the man he'd hired to play Santa, had such a speech in him. After the speech, Zumwalt's phone rang so much that he ordered it replaced. Santa said he only wanted to borrow the season for one Christmas. But suppose he decided not to give it back? What was he going to do? If he didn't take some kind of action the North Pole Development Corporation would be finished. The lawsuits. The possible jail sentences. What was he going to do? Tell the press that he'd been blackmailed? But then he'd have to tell what he was being blackmailed for.

Hundreds of tiny little lights whirled about the room, until a figure stood before him. It looked like some kind of priest. The priest walked with the aid of a staff.

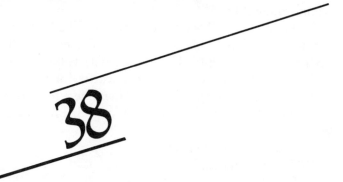

The area in front of the elevator was so lit up with man-made lights that Zumwalt had to shield his eyes with his handcuffs. Photographers from the world news media were taking pictures of Zumwalt and the two detectives walking on each side of him. They held his elbows firmly as they walked him through the lobby of the Holiday Inn. Reporters were trying to outshout each other with questions.

"Mr. Zumwalt, what's your opinion of the shoot-out in the Garden?"

"What shoot-out?"

"The shoot-out between the North Pole security men and the followers of the fake Santa Claus."

"I hadn't heard anything about a shoot-out. All these men told me was that the man who blackmailed me wasn't Rex Stuart, my employee, but an imposter."

"Now that you know about it, Mr. Zumwalt, how do you feel about it?"

"I don't feel one way or the other about it; I'm quitting as president of the North Pole Development Corporation." The two detectives and Zumwalt were pushed about by the crowd surrounding them, as they made their way to the Holiday Inn exit.

"But Congress is preparing a bill that would give your company land at the North Pole for your domed city; why would you quit now?"

"I have to beat this rap. I'm innocent. The President's son accidentally slipped. All of these years I've been on the run because of an accident." The trio was outside the Holiday Inn and headed for the detective's car when Zumwalt heard a familiar voice in the crowd. It was Jane. She ran towards him, maneuvering her way through the throng. She threw her arms around him.

"Jane," Zumwalt cried.

"Ziggie," Jane said.

"Jane."

"Ziggie."

"Jane." The detectives halted the procession and permitted the couple to spray each other about the cheeks, lips, and noses with passionate kisses. Even the normally grim-faced detectives had to smile. After all, it was the Christmas season. The detectives helped Zumwalt into the back seat. Jane took a seat in the front next to the driver. A persistent reporter fired a last question as they were about to drive away.

"What made you decide to turn yourself in at this time?"

"The hotel chaplain, I think he was. He said that it was never too late to begin again. He persuaded me to turn myself in. Nervous fellow, though. Kept moving gold balls about in the palm of his hand."

39

The White House was empty except for Bob Krantz and the F.B.I. Chief, Charles Klein, who were conversing in the Oval Office. The F.B.I. Chief's white hair was lying on his head as though it were his skin; he wore a striped tie, gray three-piece suit. Krantz sat on the off-white silk damask armchair, and the F.B.I. man sat across from him on a white couch which had been there since 1981, a very white year for the White House and for the country as well. The F.B.I. man's black shoes rested on the yellow rug bordered with turquoise rosettes. He was sipping from his china cup. The cup cost $500 in 1981.

"They made their getaway shortly after the shooting began. One of Zumwalt's men was killed and several wounded. A couple of the kids were killed. Several people were trampled as they tried to reach the exits. When the shooting began, people panicked."

"What about this fellow who says he was kidnapped by Santa and the bellboy?"

"That's the strangest story of all. He says that the imposter Santa Claus was under the bellboy's command and didn't seem to have a will of his own. When Santa and the bellboy escaped in one of Big North's limousines, an eyewitness said that the imposter Santa seemed to be limping."

"How does Zumwalt fit into all of this?"

"He says he's not guilty of murdering the President's son, he says it was an accident."

"Not that, the other. How does he fit into the scheme with the bellhop and Santa?"

"He says that Santa Claus blackmailed him. That he knew about the nose."

"What nose?"

"His nose. He had a plastic surgeon do something to his nose; Santa found out. Said the bellboy had all of the before and after photos in a neat file. He said that the imposter Santa Claus said that he wanted to borrow Christmas until Christmas Day."

"Maybe they're gone."

"The lights are burning all night at the J. Edgar Hoover Building, sir. We won't sleep until we catch those two."

"Good," Krantz said. "What else did you find out?"

"We tracked down Santa's fingerprints, the imposter one; they match up with those of Snow Man, the notorious enforcer. He was known to do some freelance work for some of the, er, black gangs, sir."

"You think that the blacks are behind the whole thing, Klein?"

"There was the black bellhop. We haven't been able to turn up anything on him."

"Blacks in some kind of conspiracy to knock off Christmas. You think maybe because it's white?"

"We're trying to gather all of the facts, sir."

"That society, what did they call themselves?"

"The Nicolaites."

"What did you say?"

"The Nicolaites."

"St. John. The Book of Revelations," Krantz muttered.

"What's that, Mr. Krantz?"

"Skip it. What happened to those people?"

"They all disappeared. Our informants said that one of

them, a Brother James, is in hiding on Sag Harbor. He's writing an eyewitness account. He's sold it to a magazine; it's supposed to be out in a few days."

Bob Krantz rose, and the F.B.I. man followed suit. They shook hands. "Good work, Klein, keep me posted on further developments."

"We should find those two in no time. They've ruined Christmas for millions of law-abiding citizens. Next year's Christmas has already begun. As soon as Zumwalt's announcement was made, a lot of unemployed Santas headed out into the streets with their bells. Pretty soon we're going to have Christmas all year around. Are you going to inform the President, Mr. Krantz?"

"No, I think I'll leave the President alone, Klein. He hasn't recovered from the news of his wife's death."

"It was a shock to us all. We checked that tree out. A troublesome career. It was a very paranoid and antisocial spruce."

"We're preparing for the worst. Might have to invoke the Twenty-fifth Amendment. That woman was like a parent to him. I'm afraid that he's not going to be able to function without her. He's useless to us now. You know, she planned to divorce him and run off with the Secretary of Defense. Our men say that this was one of the reasons the Secretary of Defense committed suicide."

"She what?"

"Sure, the rumor was all over town."

"Mr. Krantz, you're going to have to be careful about invoking that amendment. The President is pretty popular, you know."

"We'll play it on television and soon the public will swallow it."

"I always forget, sir, your former career."

"Mr. Whyte will never forget that I once worked for him, and that he was my boss. He won't answer my phone calls, says he'll only talk to the President. Sure you don't have something on that arrogant Jew bastard?"

"He's Presbyterian, sir. He's as clean as a chicken after a coyote has polished it off."

"Yeah. Right."

"You should have seen Madison Square Garden after the shoot-out, Mr. Krantz. It was a mess. They're still cleaning it up." The F.B.I. man, followed by Bob Krantz, began to leave the room. Suddenly, the President's chauffeur rushed in. He was all out of breath. He was very agitated. The F.B.I. man halted. "What's going on?"

"It's the President, Mr. Krantz. He's acting real strange. I rushed here as fast as I could."

"What do you mean, acting strange?" The F.B.I. man, tight-lipped and mean-browed, looked from the presidential aide to the chauffeur. The presidential aide, Bob Krantz, was followed by the F.B.I. man and the chauffeur as he walked over and perched himself on the desk introduced to the White House by J.F.K. The oak beams used for the desk once belonged to the British ship *Resolute*, which had been abandoned near the Arctic. "Is he drinking?"

"He says he's stopped drinking, sir."

"Stopped drinking? Stopped drinking? Why, everybody in town knows he's a fall-down drunk." The F.B.I. man laughed.

"It's not drinking, it's not drunkenness, it's more serious than that."

"What is it?"

"It all started this morning, sir. He came downstairs from the family room real early and he'd bathed and shaved, which was strange because his wife used to do that for him. He looked ten years younger, sir. Vibrant, skin looked as if he'd just come in off the beach. He started cracking jokes left and right and told us that we could all leave since it was Christmas. But then he wanted me to drive him to John's house."

"Who's John?" said the Presidential aide.

"O, he's the White House butler who's been serving the President the last few years, sir. Don't worry about him. He's as neat as a kosher kitchen. N.A.A.C.P. Contributes to the heart fund. Three generations of good church-going, upstanding folks. A.M.E. Zion church."

"A Zionist?"

"Not exactly. They're a very proud group," the F.B.I. man said. "When the whites segregated them from worship, they walked out and set up their own church. Enterprising, hardworking folk."

"Then what's wrong with the President going to John's house?"

"Well, that's not so bad, though I did feel rather uneasy opening the car door for him."

"What do you mean?" the Presidential aide, Bob Krantz, said.

"He sat in the back with the President, sir. The President had me drive to a department store, and I told him that it was Christmas Day, but the President made me call up the manager, and the manager interrupted his Christmas dinner, came down, and let the President in."

"That was nice of him. What happened next?"

"Well, the President bought gifts and made the manager wrap them. Then he had me drive him and John to John's house."

"What happened next?"

"He had dinner with John, John's nephew and two of the White House maids, Joan and Esther."

"It doesn't sound serious to me," said Bob Krantz.

"That's not so serious, I agree," the chauffeur said, "but what I think you ought to know about is what he said when he came out."

"He began to mumble awful things about Nelson Rockefeller, Dwight Eisenhower, and Harry Truman. Said that Harry Truman allowed himself to be talked into committing one of the most diabolical, heinous acts ever committed and that he wasn't going to spend his life in some first world behind a yellow wall, with dreams of white flashes and burning cities. He said that the dropping of the bomb on the Japs was an insult to God and to nature. He said that Truman should have asked the scientists—who'll do anything for fame—more questions. He said that Truman was always ashamed of his Missouri background and was afraid of intellectuals and scientists, when he was one of the sharpest intellectuals ever to serve in the White House."

"What's wrong with that? I'm not so fond of Harry Truman, the arch-liberal, myself. And maybe Harry Truman was wrong in dropping the bomb on those who would become one of our staunchest allies. If there isn't anything seriously wrong with the President, I wish you'd leave. So he has opinions. He'll never try to put them into action; he's too tired, anyway. Those expensive balls with those rich friends of his, dancing to 1940s band music, and telling famous stories from the ad business. The guy's been selling products so long that he has the dignity of the sleaziest whore. With all of that makeup on he could be a stand-in for Jezebel." The F.B.I. man and Bob Krantz chuckled.

"But there's more," the Secret Service man said. The F.B.I. man cast a cutthroat eye at the Secret Service Man as if to say, *Why is this guy taking up all of this time for nothing?*

"He said that he had enough information on both of you to send you to hell in a Concorde, and that after his speech—"

"His speech. What speech?" Krantz said. The F.B.I. man held his exit.

"He said that he's going to get Mr. Whyte to grant him TV time, and that he was going to make a speech which would take some names and kick some asses, and he said that he was going to flay away at you two especially. He said that he was going to write the speech himself because he didn't trust anybody in the White House. He said that just because you bought him a ranch and a lifetime complimentary guest room at any of Roy Rogers's hotels didn't mean that you owned him and that you could take back the yacht, the clothes, and the five-thousand-dollar gold-plated inlaid cowboy boots."

"What else did he say?" the F.B.I. man asked.

"He started to say something about Two Birds, something about a plan hatched—an Operation Two Birds." Krantz stiffened.

"Must be out of his mind," Krantz said nervously.

"He said that his speech was going to deal with that. That he was going to call for complete and total disarmament, and that he was going to nationalize big telephone, big energy, big development, and that he was going to turn the Rockefeller and DuPont estates into homesteading regions."

Bob Krantz's knees felt weak. He grabbed his throat. "Bob—Mr. Krantz, what's wrong?" the F.B.I. man asked.

"He said that every man and woman should have theoretical as well as substantive rights. The right to exist, which means the pursuit of happiness, as well as the right to eat, because with an empty stomach, pursuing anything is impossible," the chauffeur said.

"Where is he now?" Bob Krantz asked.

"The Holiday Inn." The F.B.I. man was confused.

"He said he wouldn't return to the White House for all the tea in Japan. He said one could smell the rank smell of our history behind those pure white columns and walls. He said that it was a settler's mansion, a plantation with rooms concealing lurid memories, and that it was built on the bones of blacks and the blood of injuns. He said that Eisenhower haunts its corridors bumming cigarettes. J.F.K. sits in a bathtub, wearing the tall hat of his inaugural day and smoking a cigar, meditating on what might have been; he said all of the intense violence and tragedy is holed up in here and that even Holiday Inn was a pure delight in comparison with this place resounding with the wails of Mrs. Warren Harding, and he said if they thought that what Thomas Jefferson did to Sally Hemmings was immoral, wait till they discover that he was a robber of Indian graves."

"He's out of his mind for saying that, Klein," Krantz said, "get the F.B.I. over to the Holiday Inn; I'll get the Twenty-fifth Amendment papers drawn up; you meet me there." Klein hurried from the room.

"What time is he going on the air?"

"Nine P.M."

"That's forty-five minutes from now; we'd better step on it. What's your name?"

"Tom, sir. Tom Drake."

"Go bring up the car, Tom. You'll go with me. By the way. You seem to have memorized all the President's remarks. You have an amazing memory."

"Not at all, sir. I taped the whole thing on the car deck."

"Hand it over."

"I don't think so, sir."

"Why?"

"The way I look at it, it's the most historical document since the resignation of Richard Nixon. It should be worth a lot."

When the news got around John's building that the President had had supper with John, Esther, Joan, and the little boy, James, John's neighbors began to arrive at John's apartment. It was the most exciting thing that had happened in the history of the neighborhood. John had returned to the White House to pick up some scotch the President always kept on hand in the Oval Office. Since the President had sworn off booze and become a teetotaler, John didn't think the President would mind if he helped himself to a few bottles. He put his hand on the doorknob right after the President's chauffeur had arrived and heard the chauffeur discuss the President's activities with Bob Krantz and the F.B.I. man, Charles Klein. He knew Bob Krantz as a man who wouldn't give the black White House staff the time of day, but he was always on Reverend Jones's television hour talking about how the Lord guided him in making the tough decisions of government, and how he often talked to the Lord and received instructions from Him. John was now in a cab rushing to the Holiday Inn to warn the President of his impending arrest. When John got off at the President's floor, he was stopped by a Secret Service man.

"O, it's you, Uncle," the man said. "What do you want?"

"I brought the President the slippers he requested." John stood erect and confident, still in fine shape at sixty. He let the "Uncle" go because he'd learned that the best way to grow sores on your intestines and stomach was to react to every dumb insult made by ignorant people. The Secret Service man looked into the bag and saw two slippers with the presidential seal on them.

"OK, you can go," the Secret Service man said. John knocked on the door that led to the President's suite. The President answered. He was in a robe and pajamas. He'd just bathed and shaved. There was a pile of papers next to a typewriter that rested on a desk. "John, what are you doing here? I told you to take the rest of the day off. Incidentally, that was a great dinner. Where'd Joan get the recipe for that chicken and corn? I've never tasted anything like it. Come in, John." John entered the room. "Take your coat?"

"Mr. President, your life is in danger, you must—"

"John, I want you to hear some of the speech." Dean Clift went over to the typewriter, collected some of the papers. "I wrote this speech myself, John. It came from the heart. Nobody wrote it for me, John. You know, I'm not bad. It's not too late for me. Today, for the first time in my life, I feel like somebody. I am somebody. All my life I've had people do things for me when I wanted to do them for myself. My mother, my father, everybody gave me a charmed life. Well, you know, John, you tend to be soft if you've had a charmed life. And now I know that there's something within me, something that hasn't been developed, John, you know I've never realized myself—"

"Mr. President, we must—"

"'Tonight I come before you to, as a friend of mine might say,' that's you, John, 'take some names and kick some asses and there are enough assholes in this town to keep my toes busy for some time. The problems of American society will not go away by throwing Christmas candy at them.' Clever, huh, John? Christmas candy. 'Nor will they go away by invoking Scroogelike attitudes against the poor or saying humbug to the old and to the underprivileged, nor will they go away by hatching diabolical and evil secret operations like this Operation Two Birds—"

"Mr. President, we don't have time."

"John, you don't like the speech? I worked hard on it. Listen, there's more."

"Mr. President, Bob Krantz and the F.B.I. are on their way over here to arrest you and put you away. They're going to put you in the same sanitorium as your daughter; they're going to say that you were so grief-stricken by your wife's death that you went to California for an extended vacation."

"California. I hate California. John, have you been drinking?"

"Mr. President, I heard them. Your driver told them everything. He told them about your speech and your dinner with us. When I left the White House, Bob Krantz was on the phone to Colorado, reporting to his bosses about your strange behavior and what he was going to do."

"His bosses, what do you mean, his bosses? I'm his boss."

"Mr. President, everybody in the White House knows that you don't run the government, and that the Colorado gang is in charge. We all receive our payroll checks from a Colorado bank."

"John, this is confusing; you're not serious."

"Mr. President, will you get it through your thick head

that all they wanted to use was your model's face. They know that America gets butterflies in the belly over a pretty face. It was just your face, Mr. President." Dean Clift walked to the kingsize bed as if he were in a daze. He sat down, slowly.

"Mr. President, you have to deliver that speech now. They're on the way over here."

"I'll get dressed."

They headed down the back stairs until they came to the basement garage. They jumped into John's old Dodge and headed towards the television station. Just as they turned the corner, the limousines carrying Krantz, the F.B.I., and the Washington police pulled up in front of the Holiday Inn. They'd brought an ambulance along.

*Channel II (Thriller) * * "Devil's Web." Diana Dors, Ed Bishop. A tale of menace, mystery and suspense as a nurse spins her satanic web attempting to take possession of the souls of three beautiful sisters. (90 mins)*

Saturday was at home, watching television, when the newsman broke in. "This Just In," flashed across the screen. Saturday drank from a glass of California Riesling. "For more on the shoot-out between Santa Claus forces and those of North Pole Development Corporation, we take you to Madison Square Garden," the newsman said. People were walking about dazed, blood streaming down their faces. Some were lying on the floor, moaning. Others, bandaged, were being led away by friends. Those who were not so fortunate were being given last rites. Rescue workers raced about. A reporter stood in the middle of the chaos.

"There's still much activity down here, the scene of a tragic shoot-out between two groups, apparently fighting for the control of Christmas. Ladies and gentlemen, this has got to be the weirdest story I've ever reported. As you know, Rex Stuart, one of the former stars of 'Sorrow and Trials,' revealed that the Santa who came here to the Madison Square Garden for the Annual Christmas Ball was an impersonator who had kidnapped him. He said that accompanying the man was a black bellhop who was in on the whole operation." Nance Saturday held the corned beef sandwich at the opening to his mouth. *Body Snatching!* "He said that he was held prisoner by the Nicolaites, a local cult which believes that St. Nicholas is God. Its leader is Boy Bishop, the playboy priest, who was excommunicated from the Roman Catholic Church for his overenthusiasm for Nicholas, whom the church has declared moribund." Nance Saturday stood up.

The anchor reporter appeared. It was Virginia. She'd gotten the job. "Thank you, Larry," she said to the Garden reporter whose face had disappeared from the screen. "Larry mentioned that Rex Stuart, the former soap opera star, now employed by Big North as Santa Claus, broke the story about the imposter. Your reporter interviewed Rex Stuart in his Plaza hotel room early this afternoon. He has been pursued by talk show hosts and reporters all day, and only agreed to the interview after our promise to make it short. Mr. Stuart has been in seclusion since his release." The screen showed Stuart sitting in a chair. He'd put on a little weight and was getting some color back into his cheeks. He was wearing dark shoes, white pants, and a blazer. His shirt was blue and the ascot was striped. Virginia was sitting across from him, grinning. Stuart had a twinkle in his eyes.

"It must have been a terrible ordeal, Mr. Stuart; how long did they hold you?"

"From the last Saturday in November until now. I'd just returned from a meeting with Mr. Zumwalt and Congressman Kroske. They were talking about plans for the domed city at the North Pole. I was relaxing in my room when there came a knock on the door. I opened it to see a man who was dressed like me, in a Santa Claus outfit. He was accompanied by a black man—a short black man who was dressed as a bellhop. He held a gun. I thought it was a joke until the dirty, evil little bastard began knocking me about. Twice during the ordeal at the hotel the false Santa fainted, or seemed to collapse, and both times he was revived. The bellhop gave Santa a bottle. It had a nipple on it. Like the kind you'd give a child." Virginia crossed her legs, and Rex Stuart took a quick glance at her knee. Sometimes it was hard to concentrate on her show; she wore all the latest fashions lent to the program by some of the biggest designers in New York.

"How awful. What did they do next?" Virginia asked.

"The little black man made me help him carry the Santa Claus into the bedroom and lay him on the bed. The man was dead weight, like a corpse or something. He seemed to be ill and his face had a yellow tint."

"He left the Santa in your room?"

"That's right, and he locked the bedroom door. He then made me go to the garage with him. When I got into the car he made me put on a blindfold. There were other people in the car. I couldn't quite make out their features. They wore hoods and their eyes were in the shadows. Somebody hit me on the head. When I came to, I was in a room in the basement of the mansion."

"This was the mansion that belonged to Boy Bishop and his followers?"

"That's right. I remained in that room until I managed to get free. The mansion was deserted. The place was filthy and there were crazy slogans on the walls."

"What kind of slogans?"

"I've written a couple down." He removed a piece of paper from his pocket. "Swallowfield Will Be the Battlefield, Stand Firm, and there were some horrible things written about Queen Elizabeth which can't be repeated on the air. There were some crazy paintings on the walls."

"What did you do next?"

"I returned to the Holiday Inn and reported to Jack Frost, the North Pole Development's security head."

"And what did he do?"

"Well, he went to the Garden to take care of the impersonator."

"And we know what happened to Oswald Zumwalt, the president of the North Pole Development Corporation. He turned himself in for the murder of President Dean Clift's son."

"One would have never known that Oswald Zumwalt was capable of murdering someone. He was a hard customer to please and work for, but murder, I just don't believe it."

"There have been rumors ever since you got the job that Oswald Zumwalt abused you. How can you be so supportive of him?"

"He needs my support now. He's in trouble. He's not the worst person in the world; he's just been tormented by the secret he's been carrying with him all these years. Besides, I'm through hating. I don't even hate the horrid little bellboy. In fact, I'm in his debt. Those lonely days in that basement room brought me in contact with myself. I don't hate anybody. I love everybody. Merry Christmas, everybody." Rex Stuart waved at the television audience. Virginia smiled, broadly.

"What are your plans now?"

"Sidewinder Publishers has offered me a three-hundred-thousand-dollar advance to tell the story of my years as Santa, and the inside scoop on my imprisonment. So everything worked out for the better, I think. And, Virginia, if you ever get tired of your job," he looked her up and down, "you can always come and work for me. I could use a fine, healthy thing like you."

"I might take you up on it," Virginia said, giggling. Nance turned the TV off. So that was Black Peter's body-snatching plan. Replace the North Pole Development's Santa with one of his own. *Snow Man!* But why would Snow Man go with Black Peter? Nance hadn't paid too much attention to the furor surrounding Santa's speech, but now it all made sense. They said that Black Peter was capable of imitating any famous white man and a few who weren't so famous. And so he was speaking through Snow Man? Snow Man was a corpse revived by what? Tarpon Springs? Jamaica Queens had mentioned something about Tarpon Springs. Some kind of miraculous water which would heal the dead. Nance went to the table and picked up one of the books he used during his research on the case. *Saint Nicholas of Myra, Bari, and Manhattan*, by Charles W. Jones. On page 373, "In the year the Pope pronounced Nicholas moribund, an Associated Press dispatch from Tarpon Springs, Florida (18 Dec. 1969) read in part: 'The pastor and parishioners of a Greek Orthodox church say an icon of Saint Nicholas is forming what appear to be teardrops.'" Black Peter revived the corpse of Snow Man, Snow Man having burst into the Mansion to kill Boy Bishop, only to be killed himself? The tears of St. Nicholas? The tears of St. Nicholas used to revive a corpse. But this was madness. Nance began chuckling to himself at his ridiculous thoughts. He was tired and needed a drink. St. Nicholas and Snow Man. Was Snow Man the big dummy Black Peter was trying to obtain? This had to be crazy. He'd have to give up on this case. There didn't seem to be any way it could be solved. And what had happened to Boy Bishop, James, Andrew, and Sisters Suggs, Alice, and Barbara? The police had found no trace of them.

There was a knock at the door. It was Virginia. She was wearing a maroon velvet Eisenhower jacket trimmed in mink and designed by Gloria Sachs. She was wearing a fun hat and blowing a fun horn. He could tell the way she waddled that she was a wee bit tight. She carried a bottle of Dom Perignon.

"Can I come in?"

"It's a little late, don't you think, Virginia?" It was 1:00 A.M.

"I'll just stay for a cup of coffee."

"Fine. But just one cup."

"Why are you hanging holly on your door, Nance? When we were married, you hated Christmas." Nance was in the kitchen preparing a cup of coffee. She came into the kitchen and put the champagne bottle on the table. She put her arms about his neck. The uptown perfume she was wearing went straight to his balls. She was wearing an embroidered velvet dress collared and cuffed in fragile lace. Oscar de la Renta. He often wondered even now why Virginia, as black as she was, would carry such prominent Asian features. Only Chancellor Williams would know why. She was weirdly beautiful. She was a freak.

"Virginia, I don't think—"

"Can I ask you something nasty?"

"Look, Virginia, you—" She'd left her shoes in the other room and was now in her stocking feet. Her skin had that familiar black sheen. Sometimes when you looked into her eyes you saw a jaguar in there, ready to leap. She grabbed his dick. He pushed her hand away.

"Look, Virginia," he said. "I need all of my energy, I'm thinking about a problem I can't solve."

"Let me solve it for you—" She grabbed his ass and began to lean into him, her legs beginning to spread. He began to sweat a little.

"OK, OK. We'll have a drink."

They were in the living room, drinking champagne.

He raised his glass to her. "Congratulations on getting the job."

"That bitch started to cry."

"Who?"

"That Ms. Ming bitch. She said that the only reason I got the job was because I was black."

"Well, isn't that the reason?" Nance asked.

"Look, I'm one of the best journalists in the business. I'm the only one in my department with four Emmys." They studied each other.

"I'll never please you, Nance. You just want me to be underneath you, to be submissive. All you wanted me to do was clean your house and fetch you coffee, while you studied law. Then you dropped out of law school. You just didn't have what it took to make it, Nance."

"I do OK."

She glanced at the mantelpiece. There were dozens of Christmas cards on display.

"What are those?" she said, sleepily.

"Christmas cards. Some of them are over a hundred years old."

She noticed the small Christmas tree on the hall table.

"O. Portable Christmas trees aren't so new. Martin Luther had one," Nance said.

"Nance, since when did you get so horny over Christmas? Hey, I interviewed a real-life Santa today, Rex Stuart."

"Yeah, I saw."

"He was held captive by that Boy Bishop group. Weren't you interested in them, Nance?"

"Baffled is the word."

"He said that a black bellhop was in on the scam."

"Yeah, Black Peter."

"Nance, what on earth are you talking about?"

"Skip it. Look, I have a hard day tomorrow. You can sleep here if you want." He went and got a pillow, some sheets, and blankets and brought them into the room. He converted the sofa into a bed. She was in the bathroom. He went into his room and shut the door. He snapped off the light and went to bed. He left her sitting on the sofa, pouting.

Shortly, he felt strange sensations moving up and down

his veins and through his nerves, and there were tiny explosions of delight in his neck, thighs, feet, and back. He awoke to see Virginia. All she had on were yellow bikini panties. She started to move from his pelvic area towards his lips, sliding over his body. She'd really learned her way around the corporate world, all right. He could understand why snake worship became so rewarding for certain ancient peoples. She gave him one of those Russian Lilith kisses as though she were trying to suck his insides out.

"Virginia, I'm not wearing anything." She made a sound of exasperation. He reluctantly got up, went to the bathroom, and spent some time trying to get the contraceptive to fit. The third one didn't break like the other two. When he returned she was lying in bed, the yellow panties on the floor. Big-legged country girl. He remembered that making love to her sometimes was like trying to pry open a lobster with a comb during their pouting, dry marriage, but at other times it was like walking through the Holy Land barefoot. He removed his slippers.

41

There are four, three, no, two people standing at the foot of her bed. Rex Stuart and a nurse. She came around.

"No, don't move. I brought you some flowers," Rex said. The nurse smiled and left the room. He put the irises in the vase next to her bed. She tried to talk but he put his finger to his lips. The doctor had told him that whatever Vixen had witnessed had left her unable to talk, though she could write things down on the yellow legal pad that lay on the table next to her bed. Her last memory was entering Santa Claus's suite. She pointed to Rex's midsection and laughed.

"Didn't recognize me, did you? Nurse down the hall said that I looked like Gregory Peck." She pointed to the pad and the pencil. He handed them to her. "You look very handsome," she wrote, smiling. She was more striking than he ever thought, and all those times he'd passed her in the hall, not once had he taken the opportunity to invite her to lunch or to a show. "They told me at the Holiday Inn that you were trying to reach me. I guess you know about what happened."

She picked up a copy of the *Daily News* that lay next to her. The headline read: "Fake Santa." She picked up the pad and wrote: "You're very brave."

"Why did you come to see *me*? I couldn't understand why you wanted to see *me*." Stuart sat down on the edge of the bed. His yachtsman's cap rested on a chair near the door. She wrote, "It was because of the speech. I thought of your speech and that's what brought me down. But now the speech doesn't matter. You're wonderful as you are." Rex Stuart was touched. It had been many years since someone had said something like that to him.

"I had a lot of time to do some thinking down there in that basement. Scenes came from my life—they played like a jerky silent movie. I was on television. I was out of touch. You can get a swelled head from television. Reaching more people at one time than most of the authors of the last three hundred years put together. And the cable. And the satellites. And the discs. Do you know that 'I Love Lucy' show signals left earth and have reached the farthest galaxies by now? You get the feeling that you're a god. They give you anything you want in Hollywood. Limousines, coke, slaves, anything you want. But then I decided that even though I had all of these things, the television bosses had me under their heels. They were getting more out of my talent than I was. And so I agitated among the other employees for a strike. I thought that with those millions of fans they wouldn't dare get rid of me. I was wrong. The television bosses were . . . were . . . like Molochs and I was just another body for them, another leg wiggling from their mouths. Vixen, I don't have to tell you how they busted me. I couldn't get a job anywhere. I began to drink." Vixen moved her hand across the bed to his. She squeezed. "I was going downhill in a hurry and finally took the job with North Pole. Vixen, I knew what Zumwalt was up to, and I went along with it, permitted myself to be used like a big dummy." Vixen wrote down: "Me too."

"You're not as guilty as I am, Vixen. I was the product. I allowed myself to be used by the rich to rob the poor of their Christmases. The kidnapping is the best thing that ever happened to me." Vixen wore a puzzled look. "How so?" she wrote.

"I was alone. I was able to think, and I had a vision."

"A vision?" she wrote.

"I was thinking. I would spend lots of time thinking and sleeping. I wouldn't eat the food my captors wanted me to eat. I was fasting. I began to realize that buried underneath all of this fat was the real me. Well, they say that when you fast, your buried senses, the senses you don't use, which were once used but long ago fell into disuse, like the appendix, become active. Saint Nicholas came to me, Vixen. He had on this real elegant bishop's headdress, and he carried a very ornate cane, and he wore a robe that was of such brilliance it lit up the room. He said that I didn't have to wait until death to get going, that there was plenty of work I could do in this life. You know, I always thought that Saints were solemn, but Nicholas had a real sense of humor. He said that I shouldn't wait until death to make a name for myself, the way he did. He said that a legend could be defined as someone who had to die to find himself. He said that I shouldn't have let my firing from Whyte B.C. get me down. That the bosses are powerful, so powerful that you can't beat them by yourself, you need help, he said that I had to organize and that the union would make me strong, and then he started to sing 'Solidarity Forever.' He said that I still had plenty of time to help people. He said that he's spent hundreds of years trying to help people, rescue people, and that he had had to move fast in order to keep up with his bones.

"We talked a lot, Vixen. It was Saint Nicholas who helped me get out of there. He said that he was thrown in jail once for slapping Arian, the priest of Alexandria, in the face for insisting that Jesus was a man like any other man. This happened at the First Council of Nicaea, where Emperor Constantine convened three hundred and eighteen bishops to decide about the divinity of Christ and the day on which Easter was to be celebrated.

"The bishops persuaded the Emperor to strip Nicholas of his garments and chain him. That night, Jesus and Mary visited him in jail and when the Saint told Jesus he had been thrown in jail because of his love for the Lord, Jesus set him free. St. Nicholas set *me* free. Then he disappeared. I know that's a hell of a story but that's the way it happened. And when I left my basement prison I found that the house was empty. That's when I told Jack Frost about the fake. Then I learned that the group had been blackmailing Zumwalt. I'm glad he's confessed. What a burden to be carrying around all those years."

She passed him a note. "I'm glad you got away."

"Vixen, I'm quitting North Pole Development Corporation. After I write my book, I plan to do something for working people. Maybe organize another union. I'm going to need someone . . . I mean, there's going to be a lot of work—" She handed him a note.

"I'd be glad to help you organize a union. When do we begin?" she wrote.

"As soon as you get out of this place." Rex Stuart beamed at his new partner. They would wage a war against the bosses, and the subzero people, the heartless Scrooges who had driven the poor out into the cold.

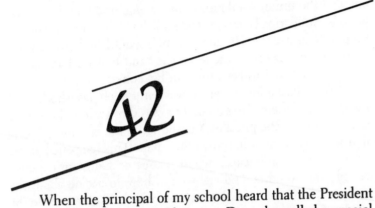

42

When the principal of my school heard that the President had visited my house on Christmas Day, she called a special assembly. There's a little girl who sits in front of me. She wears ponytails, purple tights, and pink tutus to school. She is the prettiest thing you'd want to see. I've been trying to get her attention for the longest time. So when the principal introduced me and I came from behind the curtains, I looked right down at the second row at her, and she was smiling. The other kids applauded for a long time. Some of the local Washington television stations were present and so the aisle was full of television cameras. There was so much light I couldn't see. I could see the principal, however, and while I was talking about how the President came to my house and about the gifts he brought, a man approached the principal and began to whisper in her ear. The principal waved for me to stop. She said that the man had been sent by the President, and that the President wanted me to attend some kind of ceremony with him. Hotdog! I thought. I would get the rest of the day off from school. I was escorted out of the auditorium and as I passed the seat where the little girl was sitting, I winked and do you know what? She winked back.

We drove to the White House and it must have been forty, fifty—we must have been going a hundred miles an hour, and when we reached the park across the street from the

White House I noticed that the President, Uncle John, Esther, and Joan were dressed in their Sunday best clothes. I wish they would have let me go home and change because all I had on was a sweater, galoshes, and a brown corduroy pair of pants. The President beckoned me to join him. He was holding a shovel in his hand, and his hair was waving in the breeze. It was cold but he wasn't bundled up like everybody else.

There was a little crowd gathered there and he told them that he was delighted to plant a baby spruce tree to replace the one that had burned, and that before you knew it the spruce would grow into a huge tree, and it would be the permanent Christmas tree for the nation, and that they wouldn't have to cut one down every year, robbing Alaska of its beauty. He said that the baby spruce was a symbol of a new America, an America purged of its settler past, an America that would begin its history with the landing of the red man on the North American continent. He said that when the nation was told that it was a young country, this was a hill of beans—that America was one of the most ancient civilizations known. He said that a lot of greedy people were sore at him because of his television speech, but that it was just too bad and that he was going to work hard to get his programs through and this would be the first step in civilizing a country that had been barbarized by the settlers. He said that you could tell a civilized nation by the way it treated the poor, the sick, the old, and the jailed, and that by every yardstick the country had failed in these areas.

I was asking a TV newsman when this was going to be on television, when the President called my name. He told the crowd that I was his special guest and that he wanted me to do him a favor by shoveling the first dirt upon the baby spruce tree. I gave my grandfather one of my crutches and I moved over to the President as the crowd applauded. I picked up the shovel with my left hand and held my crutch with my right. I shoveled the dirt on and the people in the crowd whistled and cheered. Then the President shoveled some dirt on and the people cheered again. The people turned their heads towards some men who were entering the park. The President, me, Esther, Joan, and my uncle looked, too. There were some police and some plainsclothesmen who were also wearing guns. A man in the lead walked briskly. He had on black shoes, black pants, and wore what my uncle told me later was a camelhair overcoat. His tie was striped. He was wearing glasses and his teeth seemed to be rattling. "Bob Krantz," I heard my uncle whisper to Esther and Joan.

The man approached the President. The President asked how he was feeling, and the man couldn't look the President straight in the eye. I noticed something strange. What appeared to be a little teddy bear's leg was sticking out of one of his pockets. He seemed to be fondling it. The President was friendly to the man. The man told the President that he was inca- inca- incapa-ci-tated, which means sick. The President read the piece of paper this Bob Krantz handed him. The marshals put handcuffs on the President and when some of the people in the crowd tried to intervene the police shoved them back. They started to take the President away, but he paused long enough to say something to me. I think he said, "Stand firm." I couldn't exactly hear. Some of the people in the crowd started to throw things at the President's captors, and when that happened one of the policemen threw a tear gas cannister. The tear gas floated our way, and so my grandfather grabbed me and Esther, and we started to leave the park. As we started to get into my uncle's car, Esther and Joan were crying. They said that it was due to the tear gas. My uncle had a tear in his eye which he wiped away. He must have been gassed, too.

My uncle said that we shouldn't worry. That the President was going through bad times now, and that he was suffering for all those times when he didn't have to suffer, and life was handed to him gift-wrapped. He said that the President had taken and now it was time for him to give. He said that his mother always mentioned an old Afro saying that he didn't understand up to the time he was about forty-five years old, and then he discovered what his mother was talking about. I told my grandfather to tell me the expression. He said that his mother told him that whenever she felt the world was giving her the cold shoulder and that winter wasn't going to let up, she always thought of what her mother told her and what her mother's mother told her mother: "Suffering is seasoning."

Class status used to be determined by which side of the railroad tracks you lived on. In 1990 New York, it was determined by whether you lived above or below the freeways which now fed into the city. The rich did all of their shopping, loving, eating, playing, and working usually above the thirteenth floor of mile-high buildings; the poor scrounged around beneath the freeways. So that the wealthy wouldn't be inconvenienced by the sight of these wretched people, a series of tunnels and monorail transportation connected the rich to one another.

Fred King lived high up. He did his business in full view of the clouds. One could see the planes land at JFK from the living-room window of his hi-tech apartment. Fred fastened the string of pearls that hung from his wife's neck. Anne still had her patrician features and carried herself in a way that denoted good breeding. Her family had a lot of money and lived in Chicago. Her father was into microchips and spoke Arabic, fluently.

Fred wore a classic black tuxedo. "What time does the party begin?" his wife asked. "Nine," Fred answered. "The Governor said that he was very eager to talk to me." He held her shoulders and kissed the back of her neck. She bent her neck to one side, and placed her palm against his right jaw. They were staring into a mirror which was decorated with a gold scalloped frame.

"I'm going to get the Senate nomination, it seems," Fred said. The newspapers carrying his photo lay on the black round table in the living room. He had been hired by Boy Bishop's family to represent Boy Bishop in the criminal charges that were being brought against the priest and his order. Boy Bishop was secluded in the home of one of his society friends. It had been decided that he'd surrender to the authorities after he had rested a bit. Fred King arranged that.

There was a huge manhunt on for Santa and the black bellhop. When the police had broken into their mansion, after Rex Stuart's dramatic reappearance, the place was in a mess. A goat and a rooster were wandering about and the walls were covered with slogans: "Babylon Will Fall" and "Ras, The Regenerator." The paintings, rich in inexplicable symbols, had been taken to the police station and put under arrest. Boy Bishop had told King that the paintings were a product of Black Peter's deranged vision and that he and another brother named James had fled the mansion after an attempt on Boy Bishop's life. The three of them had been in a meeting arguing when a man requested to see Boy Bishop in the mansion's front hall. He said that the man had fired and missed. Boy Bishop had told King that Black Peter and some of the others had captured the would-be assassin by wrestling the man to the floor. Boy Bishop also told King that he and Brother James had decided not to return to the mansion. The shooting was a sign that things had gotten out of control, and when Fred King informed them that there was a possible link between Black Peter and Rex Stuart's kidnapping, Boy Bishop told King about Black

Peter's strange plan to kidnap the Zumwalt Santa Claus and replace him with a dummy through which Black Peter would throw his voice. They had dismissed it as a fantasy, but apparently the clever black devil had brought it off. But then again, Snow Man was no dummy, and so the only conclusion that King, Boy Bishop, and Brother James could make was that Snow Man, who had been hired by some gangsters to hit Boy Bishop, must have volunteered to assist Black Peter in his body-snatching scheme, for more money than the gangsters paid him, and since he had a Santa Claus body, Snow Man became a substitute for Rex Stuart. As for the speeches and the performance, Black Peter—disguised as a bellhop—had coached Snow Man. There would be speculation about this strange case for years.

"If I get Boy Bishop off, the sky is the limit," Fred King said. "His friends are connected to all of the bigwig politicians in the state. They are the ones who arranged for us to attend the Governor's New Year's party."

Anne King looked at her watch. "Dear, we'd better be going."

"What's Junior up to?"

"He's upstairs working on his TV station," Anne said.

"That kid is always tinkering with gadgets. He'll make a great scientist one day." Anne yelled up to Fred King Jr.'s room, as her husband helped her into her ankle-length mink.

"Yes, Mom," Junior called down.

"We'll be back about two o'clock. Be in bed by then, OK? I don't want you up watching the all-night movies tonight."

"OK, Mom."

"Happy New Year, Junior."

"Happy New Year, Mom, Dad, have a good time."

As soon as his mom left, the ten-year-old put on his Air Force glasses, black gloves, leather jacket, and black jogging shoes, and went downstairs to the kitchen. Through a huge kitchen window he could see the sparkling colored lights of the other high buildings made of concrete and steel; he could see the yellow lights of the monorails and tunnels moving across the sky. He removed some rolls, potato salad, green beans, and about a third of the turkey, and a huge slice of blackberry pie from the refrigerator. He wrapped the food in aluminum foil and placed it in a plastic bag.

The guards in the lobby glanced at him, suspiciously. The guards were mostly surplus people hired to keep their own kind off the premises of these high buildings where the vital people dwelled. They were surplus people, being groomed to become vital. Their eyes remained on him until the motorcycle was out of sight. Seldom did one of the vital people come so low.

There was no sound in Fred King's apartment unless he desired it. It was still among the rich. On the street level, though, it sounded like the ragged crowds of Dickens's London, or Orwell's Paris; it sounded like Kingston, Bombay, or any other city teeming with the poor. He drove his motorcycle through the dirty hands reaching at him from the gutter, grabbing at him from under manhole covers; all sorts of garbage rained down upon him. The streets were littered with man-made and human junk. Deserted automobiles from another era, some with only their axles left. Crippled and dying buildings. He rode until he came upon a section of the city where anybody who was tough enough was the law. The young guards halted Fred King, then, noticing his Star of David, let him through. He came upon a red brick building which must have been abandoned decades before.

He entered the elevator and as he rose he began to hear the rolling, thumping music—the music of the water people, of pipes and bubbling instruments; a galloping sound was made by the drums. He could hear people singing "Santa Claus Is Coming to Town," only they were pronouncing it "Santy."

He left the elevator and walked towards the door leading to the ballroom. He knocked. The door opened and the herb smoke hit him square in the face. He could see the posters of the Emperor, mounted on a white horse. On some posters he was referred to as Selassie-Nicholas, and on others he was called Nicholas-Selassie. Brother Andrew's freckled face lit up as he opened the door for the new arrival. Andrew's head was covered with red locks. Andrew took Fred King Jr.'s contribution to the New Year's potluck.

44

Nance Saturday had returned to his apartment, after depositing ten thousand dollars in one of those high-yield accounts. He was sitting in a chair, his feet propped up on a table, watching the morning news. A psychologist was saying that Operation Two Birds was an example of President Dean Clift's paranoid fantasies, and that other parts of the speech exhibited symptoms of infantile aggression.

On another channel, Mr. Whyte, of Whyte B.C., said he had had no choice but to give the President time to make his speech. He said that he was in the studio when the President arrived with his butler, and that the President showed no signs of the condition that caused Bob Krantz to have him declared incapacitated. Whyte said that he was just as shocked as the nation was at the content of the speech; that he'd seen the President at a number of parties over the years and never thought that he felt one way or the other about politics. Another channel showed acting President Jesse Hatch explaining how the President, grieving over his wife's death, needed a long rest, and that his grief had caused him to go on nationwide television and make the shocking speech that the nation would be discussing for years to come.

Another channel showed scenes reminiscent of Douglas MacArthur's suppression of the veterans' bonus march. State Troopers were dismantling tents and tear-gassing the thousands of squatters who had moved onto the Rockefeller and DuPont estates, after Dean Clift's notorious speech. In another scene, crowds holding umbrellas and candles stood vigil outside the medieval gates of the sanitorium where President Dean Clift had been placed by the government. The manhunt for Black Peter and Santa Claus was still on.

Politics, Nance thought. For Nance, politics was what M.C.P.'s in the old days used to refer to as "a dog." Nance didn't know what people saw in her. He chuckled as he thought of the note Virginia left after spending the night at his place. The note he'd found when he returned from jogging that morning. "Thanks for letting me stay over. I must have been really drunk. I thought I went to sleep on your sofabed, but I woke to find myself in your bed. Thanks for sleeping on the sofa. I hope I didn't put you out. Will call next week about the papers." Just like Virginia, he thought. The phone rang. Nance went over and picked it up. He stood in front of the window. When he heard the voice on the other end a sweet ache swam through his body. It was the mysterious black Russian lady, whose last name included a hyphen. She wanted to know what he was doing for Lent and would he have vodka and waffles with her at one of the Russian Orthodox churches. He didn't answer right away because he was staring at a man in bishop's hat and gown who was flying above the roof of the building across the street. His speed accelerated until the flying figure was out of sight. Nance rubbed his eyes.

"Nance, Dahlink," said the voice on the other end of the line. "Are you zere?"

DALKEY ARCHIVE PAPERBACKS

Visit our website: www.dalkeyarchive.com

DALKEY ARCHIVE PAPERBACKS

Visit our website: www.dalkeyarchive.com

Dalkey Archive Press
ISU Campus Box 4241, Normal, IL 61790–4241
fax (309) 438–7422